E L L I S T O N

JASON ELIA

INSPIRED BY THE MUSIC OF
THE PINK SPIDERS

ISBN 0-615-68400-9
EAN-13 978-061568400-0

I've never seen myself as a writer truthfully.
But yet here it is; my first novel. And hopefully someone's
actually reading it. It'd be kind
of weird if I wrote this entire thing in vain.

There are a lot of people to thank,
and they know who they are. But I do
want to mention a few.

Firstly my father. We've never even been on the map of what
a traditional father son dynamic should be. But for all the
dysfunction, lack of communication, and the void of emotion,
I've never doubted that he loved me.
No matter how fucked up we are.

Next, it's Jon, Decious, Robert Ford III and Matthew Bell.
Three guys that helped foster my love of the music and
scene this literary footnote is based in. Any and all success
of this will be repaid
in endless PBR and shots of whiskey
(Jäger and Miller Lite for Matt)

And lastly, to my muse. At the time I write this
11,837 hours, 493 days or 16 months.
You've inspired the words that make it
to paper and the characters I create.

It is a blessing to know you and love you.

DEDICATION

SPECIAL THANKS

A.K. Cholewinski
Donna Cavanagh
Angela Young
Kristi Wirz
Sherry Mills
Fred Hofstetter
Justina Ellis
Kym MacDonald
Kelley Styring
And
Frank Portman

Song lyrics in Chapter 10
taken from "Welcome Home,
Kentucky"
Written and Copyrighted by
Jon Decious and Dillon
Napier

PROLOGUE

All The Cool Girls Are Dead

He stood in the hall just outside the door, his stomach in knots, his eyes red and swollen. He scratched at a thirty-six hour beard shadow. His hands shook as he reached out and tore the yellow crime scene tape from the door. He stepped back and breathed a ragged breath, and reached out to touch the closed door with his finger; he drew a heart as fresh tears filled his eyes. He stumbled back and slid down the wall behind him.

He could literally feel his heart breaking, tearing, ripping; it beat fast, then it beat slow as he cried, and he sobbed loudly.

"Oh God! Oh God!"

He wiped his face with his sleeve; hit his head back against the wall. He told himself to stand, to breathe as he slid back up the wall, his full weight against it as he prayed only to find his legs were made of no more than jelly.

Standing, he shook his head back and forth as he breathed deep, fast successive ragged breaths.

"Do it Benjamin! Just fucking do it." He whispered.

In one fast yet jagged motion, he reached out and stepped forward, his hand turning the knob. The door traveled back as he fell against the doorjamb for support. Slowly, he raised his head and looked into the room.

The morning afterglow was a dingy all white room. The sun fought desperately to make its way through dirty windows, but it found itself further diffused and thwarted in its efforts to light, warm, make merry or invade the room by nicotine-stained lace curtains.

The mint green, queen-size, princess bed, no longer adorned with its crowning canopy, sat empty and soiled in the center of the room. He avoided the bed with its vomit-stained pillow--a pillow that spoke of the hell that his eyes had opened to, too late to prevent that painted all the colors of his yesterday while single-handedly changing the course of his tomorrows.

His eyes locked on a pink CD case that rested on a 1960's child's writing desk which was the same mint green as the bed. He picked up the case as he sat in the dainty chair. The case was empty. He looked up on the shelf above the desk and noticed a CD in the player that sat there. Absently, he pressed *play* and began to cry as his own voice filled the room.

As the song ended, he once again wiped his face on his sleeve. He took a deep breath. "Pull it together, Dude. Pull it together." He dropped the case on the desk as the next song began. He absently pulled open the bottom desk drawer and began to shuffle through the forgotten memories of his love as a teen. At the bottom of the drawer, his hand found and pulled out a white, leather-bound journal.

Carefully, tenderly, Benjamin opened the cover and ran his fingers across the feminine handwriting of a girl who would become the love of his life. Through tear-filled eyes, he read the words. As he read, the events unfolded before his eyes, and he watched the demons that would haunt and stalk her until her death, be born.

There was once a young beautiful girl with smoky blue eyes named Danny. Looking every day of her seventeen years, she sat in her pearly, white room at her princess desk writing in her new white journal. White and all its shades were her favorite colors. It wasn't that she lacked imagination, rather it was that she liked clean, pure, new, blank slates. She loved subtle undertones of pearls, the freshness of snow. Clean blue lines on stark white pages. To her, white meant opportunity.

She looked up at the sound of a knock on her door. "Come in." Danny watched as the door opened and her Uncle Dean walked in with her best friend Gina Marie at his side.

"Sweetie, we need to talk."

Danny dropped her new pen onto the partially filled page of her new journal.

"What's wrong Uncle Dean?"

Gina Marie with tears in her eyes walked over and hugged Danny.

"I'm so sorry Danny."

"Sorry for what Gina? Uncle Dean, what's going on?"

Dean saw the fear growing in Danny as she both held onto and looked over Gina's shoulder.

Tears filled his eyes as he spoke, "Danny, it's your father."

"No!"

A decade in the future, Benjamin slammed the journal shut.

"Fuck!"

He leaned back in the chair and put his hand over his mouth. He gulped at air as if it were water, and he was dying of thirst. How many tears could one man have? God, he had to breathe. He had to maintain control. He had to know. He had to meet the demons. He…

Opened the journal once more and felt himself twisting and twirling back through time and space where he watched as Danny stood in the kitchen doorway looking at her Uncle Dean, who sat at the end of a long wooden dining table with a glass of Bourbon in front of him.

"How many have you had Uncle Dean?"

"None. It's not that I don't want to. I just know that it's not worth it."

Danny moved silently into the room and slid into a chair next to her uncle. "That's the one question I always wanted to ask my dad."

"Your father was a good man."

"I know."

Dean fought to keep his voice and emotions in check.

"I... I don't know what... what to say here. I'm so sorry, Sweetie." He wiped at his eyes. "You are old enough to know your father...who he was. Sometimes, it just doesn't seem right, fair, for every gift he was blessed with, he was cursed with a problem."

Danny reached out her hand and covered his. He placed his other hand over hers and looked her in the eyes. *"I really wish you had.....”*

"Had what?"

"Had a chance to know him the way I did. To know him before your mother died."

"I did know him before that; I was young... but I do remember. And I remember every time I go back and listen to his first few albums."

"It really turned to shit for him personally after that."
"Ah... But it made him professionally."

Dean looked into her eyes. *"What the hell." He made a sarcastic one note laugh sound, "Record execs used to joke behind his back about how her death was the best thing to happen to his career."*

Danny disengaged her hands and removed the bourbon glass from in front of him. "Uncle Dean, you have come too far--way farther than Dad ever tried. You don't need this."

"Sometimes, you are a lot wiser at your age than I am at mine."

"It's the one thing I can give my six stepmothers and all that time alone credit for."

"Don't ever for one minute think he didn't love you."

"I know he loved me."

"Those 300 odd nights a year we used to spend on the road--you were all he ever talked about."

Danny smiled, "I always thought his interests lay in the whores he brought home."

Dean shook his head and smiled, "Smart mouth. Listen to me: Your dad, he just never figured out how to deal with the pain."

"But you did."

"It wasn't so much that I figured it out as it was about Gina and her mother. I realized I couldn't afford to lose them when I realized how close I was to that loss – I stopped."

Absently gazing at the wall Danny slid the bourbon glass in circles. "Sometimes I wonder....."

"About?"

"What would it have been like if you and my mother had ended up together?"

"I would've been your father. And I would've ended up just like him had your mother left me still living like she did him."

"I never looked at it that way. I guess I just spent all that time envying Gina for having a father that came in off the road."

"You just remember this, little Darling. You always had me. Blood or no blood, your father and I were brothers just like you and Gina are sisters. I love you Kid."

"I love you too."

They embraced. After a few minutes, Danny spoke.

"Tell me how they found my dad."

"Sweetie," Dean said, shaking his head.

"I need to know."

"No. No. No. That you don't need to know."

"Uncle Dean."

"I know you're not that little girl anymore but…….."

"Please."

Dean looked into her eyes for a good half a minute. He saw her pain. He saw the pleading in her eyes.

"Your father had other addictions besides the bottle. You know what they were. And Darlin', that's what took him."

"Was he alone?"

"When they found him, he was."

Tears filled her eyes. "And now I'm alone."

"No, Sweetie, no you're not."

Danny looked into his eyes. She picked up the whiskey glass and downed it. Leaping from the table, she ran out of the kitchen yelling, "I can't.... I just can't."

Benjamin's fingers traced the words; he shook his head, "I'm sorry. I'm so sorry." He closed the book. Reaching up, he removed the CD from the player and put it in the case. Rising from the chair, the journal and CD case in hand, he walked to the door. He turned and looked into the room. Kissing his hand, he placed it on the wall as he walked from the room.

CHAPTER
ONE

The morning afterglow was a dingy all white room with a mint green, princess bed no longer adorned with its crowning canopy. The sunlight, trying desperately to make its way through dirty windows, was thwarted further in its efforts by the nicotine-stained lace curtains. Benjamin knocked a pack of Doral Ultra Lights from the top of a busted nightstand that matched the color of the bed, as he reached for a blaring cell phone.

Before he can flip his phone open, he wrestled his 23-year-old, undefined boyish body free of the comforter. "How drunk did I get last night?" he asked himself still bleary eyed to the mid-day sun.

Fumbling for and losing his cigarettes he muttered, "Shit." Then flipping up the phone he answered with a cotton mouth, "Hello," As he reached out once more for his cigarettes.

A woman's voice, his woman's voice, the voice of a true volatile ten answered; "Get your ass out of bed."

Benjamin mumbled, "Fuck......."

"I'm out here working for you! Now get your ass up and don't be late for work!"

She broke the connection leaving Benjamin staring at a silent phone for a few seconds before he flipped it closed, and he grunted with a half-smile, "Bitch."

With I-440 stretching East before her like well-tuned guitar strings, Danny, a petite, just-under-30 brunette with a shaggy pixie cut, touched the blue tooth at her ear while saying out loud to the wind, "He is such a dick."

She reached down and touched the custom mounted CD player which sent her forward down 440 with her father's music ringing in her ears as she watched the Nashville skyline come into view. She kept beat on her steering wheel as she maneuvered her black 66 Cadillac Eldorado in and out of traffic with ease.

Danny sang as the wind whipped through her hair. The sun, the air, made it a perfect day to drive with the ragtop down excising the demons that plagued her today of days.

******

Danny cruised her land yacht down West End Avenue. The traffic was blissfully light, and she remembered that it was some sort of holiday, Labor Day maybe. Holidays meant little to her. She found herself almost speaking this thought aloud.

"It's a sure sign of insanity, talking to yourself."

"Well I was just talking to myself that time." She grinned as she expertly parallel parked her twenty-foot baby into two parking spaces at an angle.

Travis, a boorish balding man, sat at a table on the sidewalk of the café and looked up to see Danny park and laughed as she jumped out or rather over the passenger door. He chuckled to himself as she fed the two parking meters her car's length covered.

Danny looked up and saw him. She waved and hurried across the street. Travis thought that one day she would have to learn a lesson about jay walking. He just hoped that it was not from the back of an ambulance.

Danny rushed up to Travis who stood just in time to receive one of her powerhouse hugs.

"How are you Travis?" she asked as she moved to sit in the chair as he pulled it out for her.

"I am doing just fine….. I had almost given up on you."

"You know me when I'm flying down the interstate with my daddy's music playing. I just get all lost in time and space. It's like he talks to me."

"Yes, yes I know. You are looking good today, Danny as always it is good to see you again."

"Cut the crap, Travis; you know that I am a pain in your ass."

"I can't argue with the truth, lady."

"Hey…."

They both politely smiled. He looked closely at her and could not help but see the pain that hid just behind her bright pink smile. His heart melted just a little each time her sadness hid behind it.

He cleared his throat, "I would love to stay as I had planned and visit for a while but I have to get back to The Scene. I just wanted you to know that I have lined Seth up to be there Wednesday night at eight."

"Isn't Seth your principle to go to for restaurants and leisure?"

"He really wants to cover music. It is what this town is built on. Besides, he is the best I can offer on such a short notice. All my other writers are tied up that night. Now if you would rather wait…………"

"No, no. Seth is good. I've read a few of his restaurant reviews. Besides, who am I to argue with the likes of you?"

Travis saw the playful fire rise in her eyes and smiled, "Ha! You are the queen of arguments."

"And you, kind sir, have known me far too long."

Travis sighed as he remembered the night of her birth. "Your father was truly a good man, and he raised one hell of a daughter."

"He cast one hell of a long shadow that is for sure."

"He did so for all of us," Travis said getting to his feet. He looked down at Danny and tousled her hair and smiling, he said; "Love you, Kid."

Danny watched as Travis walked away. Her eyes filled with tears as she watched him walk down the street. By the time he was out of her sight, her tears were gone.

She took out her cell phone and scrolled through her contacts. Finding the name Rob, she pressed *send* causing her blue tooth to flash.

"Hey, this is Danny. I just spoke with the editor of *The Scene* and you have a writer coming Wednesday night."

"Really? Thank you so much. You really are amazing."

"It is just my way of thanking you for what you did for me, Rob."

"Hey that was no problem at all. He's doing such a great job; I can't believe that I am not paying you a finder's fee."

Danny laughed. "Hey Rob, I want to thank you again for taking the place over. And I know that you are well on your way to bringing it back to its former glory."

"That was never a problem, and it is I who should thank you for offering it to me. And no one--and I do mean no one--will ever know the story unless you want them to.........Hey Babe, I'm sorry to have to cut you off but the audio guys are here."

"I understand. I will see you Wednesday."

Clicking the end button on her phone she smiled as she jay walked once more to her car.

******

Moving on autopilot, his head throbbing from too much of the night before, Benjamin swung open the old Tiffany inspired, glass-paned door. The afternoon sun shined a path before him into the musty bar. Give a building forty years of beer, whiskey, cigarettes and sweat and there was no ridding it of that distinctive bar odor. He wished they bottled the scent. As the door closed behind him, he removed his oversized white sunglasses and walked along the short corridor into the bar. Rob looked up from where he stood behind the bar; he smiled as he picked up the bank's deposit bag and moved toward Benjamin.

"Hey, Benji, Benji. Good to see you, bro. You are just in time for some really great news. I just got off the phone with my girl, and she's hooked us up with a reviewer from *The Scene* for the official reopening."

Benjamin's eyes lit up; the watts in his brain began to move as he shut off the autopilot. "That is great news, Rob," he said, taking great pains to control the tone and emotion in his voice. He managed to keep any traces of excitement out of it.

"You bet your ass it is. Just make sure you get some great talent up there on that stage. Wednesday night is the night we go from dive to something slightly better."

Benjamin felt nothing short of euphoric glee, and he struggled to maintain his normal cocky tone. "No problem. Just say it and it is done."

"Just remember, Benjamin, we are about finding the next big thing so that we can say they played here first. That always brings in the out-of-towners in the future." Rob patted Benjamin on the back. "I am off to the bank." Walking toward the door, he turned around and shouted, "Drink some coffee and wake the brain."

Benjamin turned to face him and squinted as the sunlight poured through the door. "I'm wired man, just got my wheels turning."

Smiling, Rob walked out the door. Once on the sidewalk, he took out his phone and hit one number and said, "It's done Danny; he's moving for it even as I speak to you."

Inside the bar, Benjamin looked over at the stage as he walked to the bar. He had thought this moment would take weeks if not months to set in motion. His hand went to his pockets in search of his cell phone. He cursed silently to himself as he realized that he had once again forgotten it. He broke into a jog toward the bar. He snatched up the receiver of the corded phone from behind the bar and dialed a number from his memory.

The other end is picked up on the second ring. "Hey, Nate, we are playing a show Wednesday night."

In a sleep-fogged voice Nate replied, "What? Where?"

Wired for sound with his mind racing, Benjamin could no longer control the tone of his voice. Now, he just fought to control the flow of his words. "We are playing a show here, at The Muse, tomorrow night. Get a hold of everyone and let them know."

"Okay, sure."

"Hey! Before you hang up."

"Yeah. What?"

"That band *Oliver's Army.....*"

"The one from The Spring Water?"

"I need their number as quick as you can get it to me."

"Why would you want their number? They sucked a rat's ass."

"Yeah, I know. I will explain it to you later. Just call me back with the number here at the club ASAP."

"Got it."

Benjamin tossed the receiver back onto its cradle and darted into the office at the other end of the bar.

Trying the door, he found it to be locked. He cursed Rob and struggled to get the key from his tight jeans. In doing so, he dropped the keys twice before he fit one into the lock. Once into the office, he raced to the desk and shuffled through a pile of papers until he found the date book. As he was about to leave the office, the phone rang.

"Muse."

"I got the number. It's 615-555-1496."

"615-555-1496," Benjamin repeated as he jotted the number down. "I'll call them after I get Wednesday night's bands canceled."

"Dude, what the fuck are you doing?"

Benjamin dropped the receiver in its cradle without answering.

******

Danny sat with her childhood friend at the Frist Center café. The two made a striking pair. Danny, tiny, her short brown hair dulled her baby doll- like qualities. There was a fragile nature that surrounded her. Gina Marie on the other hand was a classic blonde, southern belle whose vivid blue eyes matched that of the sky on a clear sunny day. There is nothing fragile about Gina Marie's appearance but when she smiled, there was a whimsical grace about her. Beautiful and sultry, she emanated an unknowing confidence.

They sat in the autumn sun sharing a grilled Portobello sandwich. Danny was sipping an iced tea as Gina Marie reached out and took a sip of ice water with lime.

"Danny, I worry about you."

Taking a long sip from her tea, Danny looked Gina Marie in the eye, "Now, why on earth would you worry about me? All I am asking is for some free studio time…time that would be just sitting there idle anyway."

"It's the past all over again Danny. Nothing ever seems to change with you."

Gina Marie watched as Danny reached into her purse and took out a half- pint of Jack Daniels and poured it into her half-filled glass of tea until it was once again full.

"See what I mean. You fly into the sun. Too close to it with the same types of co-pilots. Then you crash, you burn, you crawl off into a hole where you lick your wounds and then you are right back up in the sun again."

"At least I do get back up…. Sorry for the tone. Look, it's not like I haven't made you money is it?"

"It's not about the money. I don't care two fucks about the money. I have never once cared about the money. It's you I care about. It's the price you always end up paying that worries me."

"Gina, Benjamin is different.   Way different. He's driven, and he's loyal."

"Those are two qualities that rarely go together in this business and you know it."

Pain   flashed   quickly   in   Danny's   eyes. "Sometimes they do. It's just that sometimes loyalty has to be split for the good of the dream. I'm always loyal and I'm always driven."

"For others…. Look Danny, I hope for your sake, I truly hope that for your sake, that Benjamin is different."

"Why are you going to these places?" Danny said fighting back tears, as she lifted her glass with a shaky hand and took a slow sip of her fresh cocktail.

"Because you have been my friend since we sat in the same playpen at *The Shelter,* during your father's recording sessions. I love you more than a sister, and I know you better than a twin. Remember Danny, I have been there before, during and after all of them. And the truth is I just don't know if I can pull us back together again if this one ends the same as the others."

Danny looked up at Gina Marie; she tossed her head and placed her hand on Gina Marie's hand. "I hope that you know how much I appreciate all that you've done for me in those dark times. And I guess that I love the way you worry about me. But I honestly think that this time I'm the one that's different."

"Spoken like a true addict……"

"No, seriously Gina. I found the hardness. I just don't always know how to use it. But I'm learning Gina. I'm working hard to learn."

"You sound so much like your dad."

"I'm nothing like him."

"You are everything like him, and you know it."

Danny let go with a reluctant smile. "Okay, I guess that whole falling apple tree thing is true.... Now, how about some studio time?"

Gina Marie looked into her friend's pleading eyes. She smiled her own reluctant and uneasy smile. "The best and the soonest that I can give you is a four-to-five hour window Sunday morning, maybe more if *The Comfies* are late as usual."

"How early?"

"Eight to noon. Then, we are booked solid until around midnight and no, I will not pull an all-nighter. It is Sunday morning or not at all for another week. Then, it's Sunday morning again."

"Wow, you drive a hard bargain."

"Those are the best hours we have available in the free package. If, however, you would like to consider one of our other packages........"

They both began to laugh. Danny said in between giggles, "I'll have him there. And I will enjoy his horror when he finds out that the sun comes up at that hour of the day."

******

His kingdom is what would serve as the living room in a normal residence. But this, The Hollywood House, as it is so affectionately known by those in the know before it was really something to know.

The walls were papered with PBR 12 packs and a 40- watt bulb was the only sun, and it burned eternally on an old, cracked milk crate some ten feet across the room from what passed for his bed that lay in front of an old fireplace. The bed was nothing but two lumpy mattresses piled one on top of the other, and it accounted for eighty percent of the furniture in his room.

Lying face down in his nest of a bed, his bare ass exposed, was Harris Tweed. Old sheets feathered his bed and twisted around him while his Buddy Holly glasses sat on his forehead.

From a muffled distance, he heard the ring tone of LFO's *Every Other Time*. Groaning, Harris, who was a short, dumpy teen of almost twenty, pushed his glasses down over his eyes and made inhuman,grunting noises as he groped around the trash and loose change that filled the floor around him in search of the phone that had stopped then started to play its song again. Remembering that the phone was in his pants pocket, he tried to crawl to the end of the bed, but he became tangled in the not-so-loose sheet and fell forward off the mattress cracking his elbow on the old hardwood floor. He muttered an obscenity and grabbed his pants.

The phone stopped its song again, and he emitted another curse as he pulled it from the pocket. He crawled back onto the top of the bed again, just as the phone started to sing again.

He flipped it open, "What! I hope you intend to give me combat pay, ye of who don't leave voicemail!"

Benjamin who has been hunched over the old-fashioned, corded phone at the bar for the past 20 minutes dialing the number over and over, laughed to himself as he pulled his voice into a superior tone. "Is this Harris Tweed? Of *Oliver's Army*?"

"Yes, it is Harris Tweed you condescending asshole."

Again, Benjamin laughed this time out loud. "Sorry about that, but I had to speak to you now and not later."

"About what that couldn't wait? Who the hell are you anyway?"

"I'm Benjamin. I do the booking for The Muse here on 4th Ave in Nashville. And Wednesday night is our grand reopening. So, I was hoping that you and yours would be available to open up the night and get the crowd going."

"Just how many bands you got playing?"

"Two if you show up."

"Seems to be a small lineup for an opening."

"To be honest with you………….."

"Ain't no such thing as honest in music."

Benjamin couldn't help but laugh. "Do you want the gig or not?"

"Depends if you're paying or not."

"Of course we are paying. You'll get $50 guaranteed, plus a hundred percent of any merchandise you bring to sell and free beer."

Harris sat straight up, which awakened the half-naked blonde that had been hiding under the sheets.

"Did you say free fucking beer? Hell yeah! I'm there."

The blonde rolled over and started to play with Harris' nipples.

Benjamin smiled and said, "Be here at 7:30 sharp for set up."

"Hey man, that's kinda early………….hello?" Realizing that Benjamin had hung up, he flipped his phone closed and wrapped his arms around the blonde. "You wanna go again?"

CHAPTER TWO

Benjamin stood in the alley next to the side entrance of The Muse; he paced in front of the door nervously taking long drags from his cigarette. The rain that afternoon had ended leaving the streets shimmering in evening's soft lighting.

Grinding out his last cigarette, he cursed in a barely audible tone, "Shit, I knew that I should've picked up a few packs before I came in." Pacing, he looked down at his watch. "Thirty minutes 'til lights down............ Come on man!"

No sooner had the words left his mouth than a white 1968 Dodge work van in bad need of a muffler, screeched to a halt in front of Benjamin. The doors banged open releasing the loud tunes of vintage Merle Haggard. Out of the driver's seat popped Harris. He stopped and clumsily crawled back into the car and turned off the music and the lights while his band members grabbed their instruments.

Benjamin opened the door to the club as Harris rushed up to him.

"You must be Benji."

"It's Benjamin, and you are late."

Harris pushed his glasses up to the bridge of his nose, "Yeah, sorry about that. Dad wasn't too wild about loaning out his van on such short notice."

"Dad?" Benjamin asked truly mystified. Recovering, he rushed on; "Whatever. Just get your shit inside and I'll show you where to set it up. But you gotta rush it."

"How about a beer first?"

Benjamin looked at him in anger and confusion. As if he didn't notice, Harris continued; "You did say there would be free beer? That was a part of the deal, right?"

Leaning against the door he had been holding open, Benjamin looked long and hard at Harris. The kid had his brain running in overdrive. "You're kidding? You don't even have time for a sound check."

Harris laughed and slapped Benjamin on the shoulder. "Oh, I gotcha, while we set up, you will bring us the beer."

While Benjamin was outside trying to wrap his staid mind and nervous energy around Harris' almost simplistic single-minded, high energy; Danny was inside sitting at the bar lost in her own thoughts.

"Hey there, pretty lady."

Danny looked up and smiled at Gina Marie. As Gina Marie slid onto a barstool next to her, Danny said, "You just couldn't stay away could you?"

"Well, it's like this. Since this talent of yours is going to be eating up my studio's time and dime, I figured that I couldn't afford not to see Judas in action."

"Meow."

Both laughed. Gina Marie slapped the bar and called out, "Cervaza. Please."

The bartender called back, "Draft or bottle?"

"I'll live dangerously and take a draft." Turning, Gina Marie looked to Danny. "Seriously, I know that you trained Judas well and he is off to soaring heights. That is if he doesn't crash and burn again."

"You know that Judas handle is unfair."

"I didn't give it to him, Danny. I am just using what is out there for the world to take."

"I know. But it is still unfair."

"It's nothing he didn't bring on himself." Gina Marie looked over to the stage alive with the movement of Harris and his band setting up under Benjamin's direction. "Remember when all of this was The Hillbilly Kradle?"

Danny smiled a far away and dreamy smile. "Every time I'm here I think of Dad. He really loved this place."

"That he did…….. So does Benjamin know about your stake in this place?"

"Hell, no; Benjamin knows only what I tell him and believes only what I teach him. My past, my Daddy, they are not in the lesson plans I have prepared for him."

Gina Marie took a long sip from her mug and looked back at the stage. "Doesn't it bother you that those boys up there are like innocent lambs being led to their slaughter tonight?"

"Ahhh...... But those innocent little lambs were thirty minutes late."

"Ohhh...... That is a most definite slaughterable offense."

They both broke into a loud laughter that drew Benjamin's attention. He turned and walked with purpose toward the bar.

Gina Marie murmured, "Speaking of the slaughter, here comes Judas, the shepherd."

"Gina! Be nice."

Benjamin stepped up behind Danny and put his arm around her as he moved between her and Gina Marie. Kissing Danny's cheek he said. "Hey Babe..... You wouldn't happen to have extra smokes, would you?"

"In my purse, Doll."

"Thanks, Babe." Benjamin moved to the other side of Danny and dug through her purse.

Gina Marie looked around Danny and said, "Hello, Benjamin."

Without looking up from his search, Benjamin mumbled a hello. The bartender approached them just as Benjamin found a fresh pack of cigarettes.

"Hey, Fiction, can you take a look at these invoices before the lights go down?"

"Sure thing. Be there in a sec." The bartender walked away. Benjamin looked at Danny and Gina Marie. "Well, duty calls." He jumped over the bar and walked to the cash register.

Harris looked up from his drums and saw Benjamin standing behind the bar. Taking this as his cue, Harris jumped down from the stage and walked purposefully toward him.

"Hey! Garcon! Benji! How about those beers now?"

Benjamin tried but he couldn't keep from smiling. The simple-minded persistence of Harris was somehow endearing. It had certainly gotten under his skin.

"Sure… Just remember we open the doors in five minutes, you need to be ready to play about fifteen or so after that."

"Will do Boss. I was wondering where the people were."

"No worry about the people, Dude. They are in a line just outside that door." Benjamin said pointing just behind him. He then grabbed four beers from the cooler and set them on the bar. "Here ya go."

Harris scooped them off the bar and hurried to the stage as if he were the victor returning with the spoils of war. A full smile filled Benjamin's face as Rob walked up behind him.

"Benji! Those invoices can wait. I am too stoked, so hit the lights and open those doors."

As the doors opened, Danny and Gina Marie moved over to a VIP table. As they sat down, people started to shuffle in. Danny noticed a young nerdy man with a press badge hanging from his neck.

"And that Gina Marie would be our positive review."

"Perhaps you should go sell your man."

"I prefer a more subtle approach."

Danny stood and waded through the puddles of people to stand at Benjamin's side. She reached out and grabbed his arm to get his attention. "Be ready to impress. That dork over there with the press badge is from The Scene."

"I know. I knew he'd be here tonight that's why I'm playing."

"Benjamin! I'm shocked. You have learned so well."

"Sure," he said as he started to walk away.

"Remember, Fiction I made you!" she called to him jokingly.

Without turning around, Benjamin threw up a hand and gave her the finger. A full smile came across Danny's face as she began to work her way back to her table.

******

As people filed into The Muse, Harris stood just off to the back left of the stage with his band members watching as the growing crowd moved forward, filling the tables nearest the stage. The chatter of the people was swelling to a dull roar. Benjamin slowly cut and threaded his way through the growing mass of people. He sneaked his way around and slapped Harris on the back.

Harris jumped when he heard Benjamin say, "Showtime."

Harris turned to Benjamin, "Scaring me is not cool dude." Turning, he addressed his band, "Let's do *Oliver's Army* proud you bunch of scum suckers!"

Brandishing his drumsticks above his head like a warrior heading to battle, he led his army onto the stage. Applause and a few catcalls began as Harris sat behind his stripped down drum set, consisting of only a bass drum, hi-hat, cymbal, snare, floor tom and a crash cymbal which sat in the front center of the stage. He smashed the bass drum a firm three times to bring the audience to order and stood up to the microphone and began to sing the opening line from *Bon Jovi's* "You Give Love A Bad Name", which got an enormous response from the crowd. Suddenly, as if by the magic of a muse, the applause and approval of those gathered seemed to give the funny, fumbling, young man his own set of magical skills that touched and ignited everyone gathered.

The next three covers: "B.O.B." by *OutKast, Nirvana's* "Smells Like Teen Spirit", and *AC DC's* "You Shook Me All Night Long" had the crowds standing in their chairs as Harris rushed into the crowds for sing along choruses. To cap off his stick-twirling and beer-swilling performance, Harris and his army turned to *Britney Spears'* "Hit Me Baby One More Time." Their rendition was laced with raunchy one liners and a comic routine between Harris and his bassist.

Benjamin stood with Danny to the side of the stage. His body was tight with tension. His hands were fists at his side as he watched *Oliver's Army* perform their last song.

"Well, can you beat that?" Benjamin's response to Danny was an icy look. "Hey, don't take your disappointment out on me. They were your idea."

"I don't understand. They are not playing original, and what they are playing, they're not playing that well.

She looked at Benjamin. She could see that he honestly didn't understand, much less comprehend what was happening in front of him. "It's called showmanship," she yelled into his ear. "They're not trying to be musicians. They are up there being entertainers."

Benjamin continued to stare at the stage with confusion and even a bit of awe written all over his face. When the final chord was played by *Oliver's Army* Benjamin hit the stage to help with the tear down while his band members crossed the stage to move equipment forward a bit. As Benjamin helped Harris with his drums he said sarcastically, "Nice show."

"I guess it was a good one. We either offend 'em or we please 'em. Either way, we know they'll be back next time and place we play." Carrying his bass drum Harris turned and looked at Benjamin, "They're all yours now dude."

Benjamin watched as Harris and his band moved their gear into the band room just behind the stage. He turned and helped his band.

Danny watched the exchange between Benjamin and Harris, and then she made her way to the table she shared with Gina Marie. Gina Marie looked up at Danny as she slid into her seat. "*Oliver's Army* are real showmen...... Pure entertainment."
"They are without a doubt."

"And Benjamin................."

"Hates it when a plan goes to ruin."

"It's pure karma."

The two women smiled at each other as Benjamin hits a chord bringing all attention to the stage. "Hey! We are *Fictional Silence*!" Taking a second look at his band he turned once more to the microphone. "Three! Five! Seven!" And their show began.

Halfway through Benjamin's first song, Harris and his band emerged from the band room and worked to make their way to the bar through a crowd of cheers and back slaps. By the time Harris was belly up to the bar, Benjamin was playing to half the audience he had started with. In disbelief, Benjamin watched as the audience swarmed Harris as he played out his set; he couldn't help but feel confused, hurt and yes, angry. How could anyone so obliviously prefer a mediocre cover band to an elite professional group of complete originality?

******

Later that night, which was really very early the next morning, Benjamin lay in the bed staring at the ceiling while Danny sat beside him at work on her laptop. He had not spoken at all since they had arrived home. The silence was an improvement over the ride home, which had been laced with more expletives than Danny had heard in any one 20-minute session before. To her credit, Danny had been patient with Benjamin's loud exhales and indiscernible mumbles. When his jaw popped, she looked over at him and with all the patience, tenderness and calm she could muster she said, "Let it go Sweetheart. Just let it go."

"I am one hundred, no make that one thousand times better than that crazy kid will ever be. It's just not right, Danny."

Reaching over to her nightstand, Danny picked up her beer bottle and took a swig. "Tonight, just wasn't your night.... Next time..............."

Leaping to his feet, Benjamin wheeled around looking at her, "Just who the hell do you think I am? Some little child you can manipulate?" His voice rose to a mimicking falsetto of hers as he continued, "Oh you'll get 'em next time." He turned from her and picked up his beer bottle and took a quick sip. "This was the first time and if you can't win 'em over the first time you're not likely to get 'em the next time!"

"Will you shut the hell up? It was one fucking night you giant asshole! A night you set up!" She closed her laptop and got to her feet. She moved around the bed to face him. "You have a choice to make here and now! You can either fight back by staying the course or you can let your inflated ego take you down faster than a lower Broadway Hooker goes down!"

"Like you know shit! I am through. Finished. Tonight ended me!"

"I know one thing for sure and many things for certain. You are a real fumble butt! And this house of MINE has too many bedrooms for me to have to sleep in the same room as an assholistic crybaby!"

With those words, she stormed from the room slamming the door. Benjamin threw his beer bottle and it missed the door slammed into the wall. The bottle hit the soft carpet intact and bounced. The wall was not as lucky. A hole, in the shape of a smile, emerged from plaster and seemed to mock Benjamin.

Disgusted, Benjamin pulled his cell phone from his pocket and dialed a number from his photographic memory.

"Come on you little bitch! Answer," he muttered.

His order was answered with Harris' voice mail, "The World's Greatest Drummer here. Please take your voice dump at the tone, and I'll call you back sometime in the near future."

"Hey, this is Benjamin. Meet me at The Gold Rush tomorrow. One-ish will be great. Oh, and I'll buy the beer."

CHAPTER THREE

3

At twenty-four, Conner followed his dream to Nashville. He knew that his talent would lead him on from there. He just had to keep his often times, too analytical mind out of it all. He stood next to the bus that had brought him here, feeling success crackle in the air. As the bus driver began to unload the luggage, he stepped forward and claimed his blue duffel bag, guitar and bass.

To the bus driver, he asked, "Do you know where 2ndAvenue is from here?"

Tired, the driver snapped back, "I don't know Kid. Try six blocks in either direction."

Smiling Conner said, "Thank you," and walked away.

Conner looked around him and noticed a large bearded man in a cowboy hat, with a guitar case hanging from his shoulder, looking at the arrival and departure board. He struggled toward him, "Excuse me."

The man, who looked at him, bore an uncanny resemblance to a very young Charlie Daniels. "Hey there, you look like you could use a hand."

Conner set his bag down and smiled, "That and some information would be great."

"I am more than happy to help if I can. So what do you play?"

"Some cheap acoustic my Mom bought me at Walmart. What about you?"

"I play a '68 Harmony with a starburst finish. What's in the other case?"

"It's a bass. My grandmother knew that I wanted an electric guitar. She just didn't know the difference when she bought the Warwick Infinity."

"She had great taste. Lucky you. So what brings you to Nashville?"

Conner laughed, "The same thing that brings us all here. Playing music, writing words amid like minds. My worst option was to keep living a couple hours away and never trying."

"I would say that just by standing here that you've made it farther than most."

"I would tend to agree. Now, it seems to me that I would gain leaps and bounds in my career if I could just find 2nd Avenue."

"Let me be the one to shove you ahead on your journey. When you walk out the front door there, go right a block and follow the neon signs until you're standing next to a forty-foot guitar."

"Thanks. So...... I guess I'll run into you later?"

"Maybe. It's always possible."

"Well, it's been nice." Conner picked up his bag and began to walk away.

"Hey Kid."

Conner turned around.

"It's open mic night at B.B. Kings."

Conner smiled and nodded, "Thanks again." Turning, he continued onward.

******

Benjamin sat in an empty Muse with his bassist Nathan. Benjamin had just laid out his plan for reinventing the band and thereby ensuring rapid success.

Nathan looked at him as if he were crazy, shook his head, took a chug of his beer then exploded, "No! No way Benjamin! Uh-uh! Hell, fucking no!"

Benjamin stayed calm. "Come on Nate. Seriously, what's the worst thing that could happen?"

"I cannot fucking believe you are asking me that. Have you gone certifiably insane?"

"Nathan, think about it for just a minute. Try to see the beauty of it."

"What beauty? There is no beauty in losing our credibility as musicians. That boy you are talking about is not a musician. He is an entertainer with moderate talent at best. True showmanship is style and style is something that comes with time, hard work and development. You just can't manufacture it with a sense of raunchy ass humor."

"Nathan, surely you realize that after last night we have to do something. And to do the right thing we have to rethink, recreate and restructure."

"What the hell are you talking about? We are dead on track."

"Half the audience left with the cover band! How can you sit there and tell me we are on track after that?"

"Because more than half that audience stayed with us. Because we have a fan base and a core audience that grows with every performance."

"I just think that if we add him……….."

"Let me get this straight. You are telling me that because some fat boy with coke bottles for glasses plays a few covers and makes a few cunt jokes and has a few people lining up to buy him a drink while you play our original music, you're going to scrap a year's worth of hard work?"

"I'm just saying………………"

"You do realize that if you do this, you will be turning your back on guys who've stuck with you through more incarnations than Shirley McClain?"

"It's obvious that we need to liven up our act."

"No Benjamin! We don't need anything at this point. It's you who needs to liven up your act. I don't know what your assholistic problem is, but I am tired of standing around and watching while you continually screw people over. People, who have done nothing, but work their collective asses off to make you look better than you actually are!"

Nathan stood up with such force that he turned over the stool he had been sitting on. He took several steps toward the door as Benjamin watched dumbfounded. Suddenly, he stopped, turned around and retraced his steps, until he stood face-to-face with Benjamin. Looking him in the eye he said, "Just remember this: Success--true success is a success that comes over time with diligence, faith and perseverance. That is the kind of success that lasts over time. This fucking bullshit you're trying to pull off is the same shit that litters the world and dies out in its own waste."

Nathan turned and stormed to the door and opened it. "By the way. I...we...the band: QUIT!"

Benjamin watched emotionless as Nathan slammed the door behind him.

******

The afternoon found Benjamin sitting once more in a bar. This time it was The Gold Rush that paid homage to his racing thoughts. He flipped from anger to confusion over the lack of comprehension and vision of his friend Nathan and other band mates. Of course, it wasn't the first time people had rode along with him only to turn their backs at what he thought was the ninth hour; and it most certainly wasn't the first time he found himself having to rethink and reinvent as he clawed himself ever forward.

Fidgeting, Benjamin took his cell phone from his pocket and checked the time; it was approaching 2:30 in the afternoon. Dropping his cell phone back in his shirt pocket he murmured; "God, is that kid ever on time?" Cupping his head in his hands he stared down at the bar.

"Hey man, you're late," Harris said, slapping Benjamin on the back as he slid onto the barstool next to him.

Benjamin turned his head to look at Harris, "Late? I've been here since one."

"And I, my good man, have been here since 12:40."
"Yeah… whatever. We need to talk."

Grinning Harris said, "You don't believe me do you man?"

"Look, dude, I don't want to argue with you."

"No need to. Just ask her." Benjamin followed Harris' pointing finger to a waitress who was standing just outside the ladies room adjusting her bra. She looked up and saw Harris and Benjamin looking at her. She smiled at Harris and blew him a shy kiss.

Benjamin looked at Harris in complete disbelief. "Seriously?"

Grinning Harris spoke, "So I was thinking that the next time we play together maybe you and yours should open up the show for me and mine."

"Not happening man."

"Hey, turnabout is fair play, after all……………"

"Me and mine broke up."

"Well, that sucks… But I'm not surprised. I sort of saw it coming."

"Really?"

"Yeah. I'm good like that."

"Okay, if you are good like that, tell me, why am I here?"

"I do not know, and to be quite honest with you I just don't care. I am here for the free beer. So, how about it?"

Benjamin signaled the bartender and pointed to Harris. Benjamin looked over at Harris and spoke bluntly, "I have songs, original lyrics and I can carry a tune. You don't, and you can't."

Harris took his beer from the bartender and looked blankly at Benjamin. "Well aren't you a blunt little bastard?"

Ignoring him, Benjamin rushed on, "You've got a gimmick that goes over extremely well…. But unless you find a way to take your show over the laughs and stuff, you don't stand a chance in hell of doing more than paying your rent, unless you move your venue to Zanies …….."

"Hey, beer only buys you so much…….."

"Please, let me finish. I propose that you drop the posers you play with and come play with me."

"Listen, dude; you're one hell of a narcissistic asshole. But I'll make a deal with you. You promise me that you will work on your people skills, and I will come on board with you."

"Really? You're gonna make it that simple?"

"Why not? After all it's apparent that you need me to keep you real. So why wouldn't I make it simple?"

"You've done nothing but try to fuck with my head since we met. So you have to forgive me my skepticism."

"You are screwed up pretty tight dude. That much I know from our 24-hour acquaintanceship. So I warn you that now I'm gonna make it my mission in life to fuck with you every chance I get. And I double warn you that I can find many and various ways to fuck with the human brain. I'm good that way."

The two stared at one another. Benjamin nodded, "Okay, great."

Harris chugged his beer dry and set the bottle on the bar. "We've got to go find us a bassist. I know a guy...." Harris jumped up and walked out. Benjamin looked at the empty bottle and tried to copy Harris' chug with his own bottle. He gagged before he got halfway through and set his bottle down. He stood and tossed a wad of singles on the bar and followed Harris outside.

Harris wheeled around, a cigarette in his hand, "So where are you parked?"

"Huh?"

"Your car man, where is it?"

"It's down behind The End."

"Cool, let's go to B.B. Kings."

"I thought we were going to meet your bass player."

Harris laughed, "Not my bass player. We need a good bass player and there is no reason we shouldn't get fucked up in the process of discovering fresh meat."

"And why am I the one driving?"

"Because I didn't drive; my dad dropped me off. Secondly, because you are too much in control to ever get too wasted to drive at this time of the day. So if I ride with you, I'm keeping my ass safe."

Benjamin gave Harris a funny look. "Okay. The car's this way." Together they walked up the short hill past a dilapidated building that is the home of The End and past the graffiti sprayed wall until they got to Benjamin's beat up Lexus.

Harris looked from the car to Benjamin, "Sweet ride!"

"Sure, whatever."

"No...dude...I'm serious. Anything with four wheels that actually runs is all you need. And you got four wheels with fallen class. That is super sweet."

"Yeah, right. You'll have to reach in through the back door to let yourself in; the front doors don't open from the outside."

"Now, that is cool." Harris said reaching in, "Fallen class with a secret entry. I like it."

Once they were inside, Benjamin looked over at Harris, "So tell me, what's your deal?"

"That would depend on just what part of my deal you wanna know."

"I don't know really. Just tell me something."

"Okay. You are pretty shallow."

"Me? Shallow?"

"Yeah. You. I asked about you last night. Seems you're either an asshole or a prick depending on who you ask about Benjamin Fiction."

"You can't believe everything you hear."

"Never do... My parents raised me better than that. I find out what I can until I can find out for myself."

"Well, good luck with that."

"I've always had good luck with that method. I have learned a lot. Always remember, Benjamin my new friend, that perception is the perceiver's reality."

Stunned, Benjamin eyed Harris. "Just how the fuck old are you?"

"Nineteen."

Benjamin shook his head, "Oh, God! What have I done?"

"Problem dude?"

"Yeah... you could say that. Not only have I bought you alcohol but I've even served it to you. Just whose ID have you been flashing?"

"Mine..... Relax, my dad slightly altered it for me and he's the best ever."

"Your dad made you a fake ID? How many times has he been locked up?"

Harris laughed. Smiling he said, "He'd love that reaction. Actually none. Unless you count the sit-ins and protests in the '60s and '70s."

"So are you saying that your father was a hippie?"

"He and Mom both. Complete with the bell bottoms, long hair, protest signs, and pot."

"But you're only nineteen….. That'd make them……….."

"Old? Would you call Dylan, McCartney, or Jagger old? I like to think of the folks as timeless in their sixties. They were green before green was more than a color. They're proponents of the zero population growth. I was kind of a surprise. Mom thought I was menopause."

"Still, that is so cool. Your parents were hippies."

"They are hippies, will always be hippies. Now they're retired college professors and work the guest lecture circuit."

"So, they're still married?"

"Never were. If you park over there it's free."

Benjamin swung his car into a spot in front of Fort Nashville. "Okay, so who is this guy we're going to see?"

"His name is Jared; everyone calls him 'Locker'. He plays in a band called *The Kings Leon*. They're pretty much destined to go nowhere."

"Kind of like your band?"

"Fuck you man. It's not like yours is heading anywhere."

They got out of the car and locked it up. Harris walked towards the old tattered cloth marquee of B.B. Kings. Benjamin led the way towards the front door, just in time to see that Harris had veered off to the side door and was jimmying the lock with a credit card. Benjamin stopped then, he slipped quietly into the side door behind Harris.

From a store room, the two emerged behind the bar. Harris called out, "Hey, Locker!"

Locker, a very tall well-built man jumped and turned around; "Jesus Christ, you fuck-tard! You have to stop breaking in like that. You know the main door is there for a reason." Locker pointed to it and turned back around to the paper work he'd been consumed with.

Harris led the way out from behind the bar as he said, "If I came and went that way I couldn't help myself to the complimentary bottle on the way out."

"Yeah, thanks for that. You do know that I have to explain the inventory shortages each month?"

"And that's why I diversify."

"Yeah. Yeah. You do me no favors."

"Well you do my liver many favors."

Scooping up the paperwork Locker said, "So what's up man?"

"Got something to ask you."

Turning to put the papers in a drawer, Locker said, "Surprise, surprise." Turning, he leaned on the bar, "What do you need bro?"

"We need a bass player."

"We?"

"Yeah, Benjamin and myself, we have a new project we are undertaking."

Locker looked to Benjamin who stood behind Harris, "Yeah, no need to introduce us. I know him well."

Benjamin spoke up, "Sorry, but have we met?"

"Let's just say that your reputation precedes you." Looking back at Harris he leaned in; "You know I love you man and I would love to play with you. But," he looked over at Benjamin, "I am going to have to pass this time around."

Unfazed Harris replied, "Alright man, I understand. You know of anyone who'd be interested?"

Locker looked from Harris to Benjamin, "So Benjamin, why isn't Nathan playing with you two?"

Benjamin was caught off guard, puzzled he stammered; "He's just burnt out right now and decided to take some time out for himself."

Turning back to Harris, Locker said, "And there's your answer Harris. If Nate isn't interested in playing with you two, your best bet is to find someone who doesn't know him or knows of him," he said nodding toward Benjamin. "And that won't be easy, because anyone in this town for more than seventy-two hours has heard tales."

Locker looked at Benjamin once more, turned and moved to the other end of the bar. He motioned for Harris to follow him.

"So, Locker, what's your problem with Benjamin?"

Locker grabs some bottles and starts mixing. "I hope you are listening when I say that knowing what I know about Benjamin, this new band isn't something I would advise." He slid a glass toward Harris, "Here try this. I call it, 'Alligator Piss'."

Harris threw back the liquid, "Not bad, tastes like a quality sports drink."

"Sweet. It's the drink special tonight."

"I do thank you for the heads up regarding Benjamin. But what he's offering is pretty good so I gotta take the risk."

"I understand. And truth be told, if anyone can navigate him and not get burned, it'd be you."

" 'Tis true. Charting the rivers of man is one of my many specialties." They both laugh. "But seriously, do you know of anyone at all that'd be up to the gig?"

"Not that I would vouch for..... Of course, you could always try Baby Face over there." He said pointing to Conner who was sweeping around the tables in front of the stage. "He came in here an hour or so ago, asking about open mic night. He just rolled into town, so I put him to work bar backing. Gives him a little cash."

"So, how do you know he plays bass?"

Locker started mixing another drink. "He brought in everything he owns on his back. One of those things was a Warwick Infinity. With an investment like that, I'd hope he has some bassist skills."

Locker handed Harris a shot glass; Harris knocked it back, "Shit man! What the fuck was that?!" he asked slamming the glass back onto the bar.

"I call that 'sex on the hair of a devil's dog.' "

"You should call it: Fuck It Sucks." Harris said as he tapped the bar, "Refill." Locker began to mix another, "So Lock, do you think that Baby Face over there would do it?"

"Probably.   But it might cost you." Locker replied handing him another drink.

"Like what?"

"You still have the house in Mount Juliet with the extra rooms?"

"Of course."

"You might want to offer him a room."

"Are you sure he isn't a murderer or something?"

"Could it be any worse than living with Dillon?"

"Oh…. Fuck you man."

Locker smiled at him as he sat the drink in front of him. Harris got an amused, surprised and delighted look on his face. So Locker asked, "Can you taste the ninety-nine cherries in it?"

"Oh God. You are a master of mix-logy. Thank you for giving my liver an orgasm and enabling my alcoholism."

Bowing slightly, Locker said, "You are most welcome."

Harris looked up at Locker and said, "I think that it is time I go and have a talk with Baby Face. What's his name?"

"Conner something or other. I didn't really hear anything he was saying, I was too busy staring at his bass and trying to hide my hard on."

"You, my man, are one sick freak."

Locker laughed as Harris walked back to the other end of the bar where Benjamin was waiting patiently.

"Well, my man Locker is definitely out. But that dude, Conner, the one pushing a broom is supposed to be a fucking prodigy. So it can't hurt to ask."

"And how do you know he's a prodigy?"

"I have a sixth sense for this kind of shit and my spirit guide behind the bar seconds me on it." Moving to Benjamin, Harris put his arm across his shoulder.

Benjamin looked over at Harris, "And you trust your spirit guide to know these things?"

"You know, I'm starting to see why people take you all wrong. You have no faith. Locker is one true dude. I trust him with my life, and he don't trust me with the liquor. And you my man need to loosen up and trust just a wee bit. Let's go see what this Conner has to say."

"Nothing ventured."

"That's the spirit, my man."

Harris slapped Benjamin on the back and walked over toward Conner. Benjamin followed.

Harris broke into a huge easy going smile, "Hey… My man… Are you Conner?"

Conner looked up, "Yeah, what can I do for you?" he answered looking nervously at Benjamin.

Harris waited a beat watching both men. He quickly realized that Benjamin wasn't going to speak. "My name's Harris and this is my new friend Benjamin. You have to overlook him he's a bit introverted at times."

Harris noticed that Conner seemed to relax a bit.

"Overlook him is something I can do Harris. What else can I do for you?"

"My man Locker over there, he said that you play bass."

"I do when I want to."

"Are you any good?"

"I can walk the strings and make it talk."

"Cool… We need a bassist. Do you want a gig?"

"Why me? You never heard me play."

"True. But you never heard us. Truth is I never heard us either. But I came here to get Locker to do the gig, but he's tied up and pointed you out. You have a bass and to be a bassist that's fifty percent of the requirements."

Benjamin broke into the conversation, "Of course being good is the other fifty percent."

Harris Looked over at him, "Benjamin, my man, didn't you hear him? He said he can make it talk. Only a first rate player would know, much less use that phrase."

"I was just saying…………."

"And at this point, Benjamin, with a dead line to fill, do you really have time to care about how good is good?" Turning his focus back to Conner, Harris said, "So where are you staying?"

"Actually I was kinda hoping to make enough tonight to put me up at a motel and figure all that out tomorrow."

"Tell you what I'll do Conner. If you walk out of here as our bass player, I will put you up at my place for a while."

"What if it doesn't work out?"

"At that point, it will all depend on how much I like you."

"I don't know man….."

"Locker told me you came in here with everything on your back. And there is one thing both of us know for sure. Bar backing and tips ain't gonna feed and house you in a hotel. Take a chance my man. You have nothing to lose."

Conner looked from Harris to Benjamin. "You're silent man, what are your thoughts?"

"Everything he said."

"Cool. But I promised Locker I would work the day and evening out."

Harris looked at him, then he looked over at Benjamin, "He's a man of his word," he looked back to Conner, "I like that. No problem there; I will be back later to get you."

"Cool."

"If you need me sooner than I show up, have Locker give me a call."

"Will do."

Harris and Benjamin turned and as they walked away, Harris said, "I have done you well. See Benji, Benji, Benji I took care of all your needs and even did him a solid. I got you a bass player, and I got me three free shots."

"I didn't get a shot."

"I'm the only one who worked here so I got the shots and that is all that matters in the end."

Walking past Locker, Harris shouted, "We are out of here dude."

"Use the front door, you thief."

Harris waved his hand and everyone laughed.

Once out on the sidewalk, Benjamin slipped his cell phone from his pocket and said to Harris; "Hey man, I'm gonna hang back a sec and make a quick call. Can I meet you at the car?"

"Cool beans."

As he listened for his call to be completed, he watched Harris walk away while lighting a cigarette.

Danny was seated at a table in a restaurant with Jay, a young man about Benjamin's age and build. He had shaggy dark brown hair that hung in waves framing his strong jaw line. They were talking business. When her cell phone which lay on the table in front of her began to ring, she picked it up and looked at the screen. She looked at Jay, "Just a minute Babe, I have to take this." Flipping open her phone, "Yes, dear one."

"Hey Danny, I did it."

"What did you do?"

"I have a new band."

"A new band? … What the…… I thought you were just going after a new drummer."

"There was a problem…. Nathan backed out on the new project."

"Really? That's somewhat surprising."

"Yeah… He just didn't like the feel of things… You know that overall feel."

Danny took a deep breath. "So… who have you got other than Harris?"

"Some guy named Conner. A friend of Harris' suggested him."

"What's his play list?"

"I… Uh… You know how you are always telling me I need to loosen up….."

"You know nothing about him…do you?"

"Uh… just what I've been told… but they say he can make the bass talk…"

"What language?" Danny asked.

"What? … You cut out."

"It was nothing. I look forward to meeting the new talent. And while we are on the subject of new talent, I was thinking you should add a fourth. Another guitar."

"You know I've always played with just three pieces. What's the use of a fourth? It's just another way to cut up the money."

"It'll add depth to the sound."

"What are you saying? Are you saying that my playing isn't filling out the sound?"

"No, Benjamin. No, what I am saying is it'll afford you a chance to be more of a showman. It'll make you a better front man. In the end, isn't it better and best is what it's all about?"

"Yeah... Maybe you're right... Maybe in the end the stuff you said is right... If I decided, where should I start looking?"

"No need to worry sugar, it's already taken care of."

"Excuse me?"

"I said I got someone I want you to meet."

"I'll meet 'im. But I make no promises. I haven't decided yet."

"I think that you need to start trusting me to do my job."

"Why should I?"

"You know that trusting me has always been what works out the best for you in the end."

"We'll talk later…."

"Benjamin!"

"Yeah? I gotta go."

"Just one more thing… I want everyone over to the house tomorrow for a meet and rehearsal."

"Sounds good, I'll tell 'em."

Flipping her phone shut, Danny placed it back on the table. Looking at Jay she sighed. "He's such an ass."

"Whatever."

"You know, Jay it would probably be in your best interest not to come across as a prick right now."

"Sorry. It's just the way that I talk."

"Well, start pretending you give a damn to what is said. I promise faking interest will always get you farther than stone cold indifference."

"I thought sexy and brooding…indifferent even was highly marketable."

"It has its place, but I don't buy the shit; I buy the original. And it's me you gotta sell yourself to now. Later, we'll sell the package to the poster set." Danny took a long slow drink and looked deeply at Jay. "Now, as I was saying before we were interrupted. Everyone has to start somewhere. That's why I am putting you in Benjamin's new project."

"It's not like he wanted me."

"He's not too keen on wanting himself. And he is my problem not yours. You being a part of this project is not conditioned on him welcoming you with loving arms."

"But........."

"It's not about Benjamin. It's about you. And this gets your name out there. When you have paid your dues, you can move on."

"And what happens if Benjamin's new project is a success?"

"It won't be."

"How do you know that?"

"I've been with Benjamin for a long time. Make no mistake, he's destined for the kind of success you need to be associated with. But Benjamin's ability to maintain a relationship with anyone for the extended period of time required to keep the success, is something he is not capable of. It's just not gonna happen. But you, my beautiful man, need to sing a hit before you're looked at to write hundreds of them for others."

Jay tilted his chair back. "So, why are you doing it this way? I just can't see how being a part of a failure is going to work out to be the best thing for me."

Danny took a deep breath, "Benjamin may not have a good name among other musicians, but his name among club owners and label heads about town is golden. When the day comes for you to be on your own, both of those things are going to help you."

Leaning into Danny, Jay took a sip of his drink. "And how do you figure people's love and hate of your man is gonna help me?"

"It puts you in the best position with the other musicians, because they know Benjamin's way and are automatically gonna side with you and welcome you. As for the club owners and labels, it's credit by association. Since Benjamin's a stand up, show up and retentive professional in their eyes, you will be to if you can survive to a burp of success with him. Trust me Jay, doing it this way may sound cold, but it'll move you along quicker than trading on nothing. Am I making sense?"

"I'll be honest. There's a part of me saying this is the wrong way to go about it. But there's also a lazy part of me saying, "Hey, let's do it." And I've never really been on for hard work and all that bullshit... So where do I sign?"

Danny laughed, "I don't do a lot of paperwork. I go on good faith." Danny stood up and gathering up her purse she leaned down and looked Jay dead in the eye. Leaning in close she said in a very low voice; "Just remember this, every person you see playing for tips on the street corners downtown, who has been in town longer than a month or so, are there playing in the streets because of me. So don't screw with me." Kissing him on the cheek she stood up straight.

Jay laughed nervously, "I kinda feel like I'm making a deal with the devil."

"It was all your choice, Darling. I'll text you the address and time for tomorrow later on tonight."

Turning, she walked away leaving Jay sitting at the table as a waitress walked up from behind him and set the check in front of him. He laughed.

CHAPTER
FOUR

4

At dusk, Harris swung his father's old Dodge van into the long drive of what was once a lavish, white, Greek revival. A hundred plus years ago when it was built, it would have been a lush mansion centered as it was on a sprawling estate. That estate over the years had come to encompass what was now two old neighborhoods threatened by urban blight. Had the home been well maintained, it would have shined as a symbol of comfort and success. It might have given off an air of happiness. As it was, the house spoke of broken spirit and screamed for the attention it needed.

Harris rolled slowly up the driveway as the shadows of early evening played in the branches of overgrown shrubbery. He pulled to a stop behind Danny's '66 Eldorado.

"Cool, my van is newer than her car."

"But your van lacks the class."

"My van has more rust."

Both men laughed.

As they were getting out of the van, Harris looked at the house where lights blazed from every window. "If I had known this was where Benjamin was staying, I'd have offered you a room here."

Conner looked up at the house. "I don't see anything so special. Your place is just fine."

"Good you can stay there, and I'll move in here."

They both slammed the doors at the same time. Conner tried to open the van's sliding rear door. Harris rounded the back of the van, "Hold on. You're going to break it. There's a trick to it." Taking over the handle, Harris demonstrated as he explained, "First, you pull it up, then you have to push forward as you pull up. Now, you hold it for a bit before you pull down while sliding. And Presto! It opens... most of the time."

Conner shook his head and smiled as he reached in to grab his bass and put it over his shoulder. "So do you trust me to carry any of your gear?"

"Fuck yeah man. It's heavier than golden shit. I wouldn't even play the drums if I didn't get to bang 'em."

Conner smiled.

"Hey! Conner got the joke and showed some emotion. You've got to stop being so stiff man."

"But if it ain't stiff, it ain't worth much of a fuck."

"Holy golden cow shit, I do believe you actually made a joke." Harris shoved his bass drum at Conner.

Refusing to stumble under the weight, Conner retorted, "I can on occasion."

Harris grinned as he shouldered a snare, the stand bag, a tom and balanced cymbals. "Let's get to that door and knock it down because Benjamin's been known to be anal over punctuality." He slid the door shut with a loud bang.

He and Conner walked across the cracked drive and up the cracking walkway. Before they could reach the broken and separating steps leading to the front door, it swung open revealing Danny holding a brandy snifter filled with her bourbon.

"So if it isn't the wannabe-famous Harris Tweed." Danny smirked ,dazzling them with her flawless thousand-watt smile.

Harris looked up from behind Conner. "Wanna be? Just what world are you living in Honey?"

Danny turned her attention to Conner as he headed up the steps, "So you must be the famous Conner 'Walk and Talk' Lee Denton."

Conner stared at her blankly. "Call me Conner."

Danny blinked, "Too Bad. I like 'Walk and Talk'. Just follow me; they're setting up in the den." She turned her back and was gone as Conner and Harris crossed the threshold. Conner looked at Harris as he set down the bass drum down to close the door. "Who is she?"

"Benjamin's girlfriend-slash-manager. Or something like that. I saw them talking before the show I played with him. They acted a little straitlaced at first, but then a little... You know."

"So, what's her name?"

"Damned if I know. This is the first time she ever spoke to me."

Conner picked up the bass drum, "Kind of bitchy first impression."

"Makes no difference in this business."

Danny re-emerged at the doorway just as Conner and Harris had started forward, "You two coming?"

Conner shot Harris another look causing Harris to drop the witty comeback that was on the tip of his tongue. Conner moved quickly and awkwardly to follow Danny's shadow. Harris stood there for another moment. Taking a deep breath, he shifted the load in his arms and on his shoulders. Moving forward he complained, "Damn, this shit is heavy." As he began to move forward, he mused to himself, "I should have mastered the damn flute."

******

Danny entered the large open den and watched as Harris and Conner set up while Benjamin and Jay stood talking and trading lead licks as they tuned their guitars. She looked at each man and saw the symmetry of looks she was ready to market. She was putting spins on their opposing yet complimentary looks. From what she saw, she knew that there were some sparks of chemistry. If they didn't blow in a volatile mixture of insecurities, vanities and narcissistic traits; if they pulled together and openly shared their talents melting into a cohesive unit, then she just might be able to pull this off and make some of her money back. Benjamin was an expensive piece of talented ass. And while she loved him with her soul, she knew with her business heart that if he didn't return his investment soon she was going to have no choice but to cut him off. Of all the men she'd made, he was the only one who seemed to fight against being made.

Suddenly Benjamin called out, "Hey guys, did Danny already tell you the great news?"

Harris looked up from the hi-hat stand he was struggling with, "What great news?"

Benjamin looked to Danny who nodded slightly, before he said, "We're opening for *Feeble Weiner* next weekend at The Exit/In."

Harris pushed his glasses up the bridge of his nose. Wide eyed with astonishment he exclaimed, "What the fuck man?"

"I know I can't believe she got us on the bill." Benjamin said amid high fives and whoops of excitement.

Looking around at the mismatched band mates Harris was suddenly struck serious, "Dude, Dudette," he said looking from Danny to Benjamin; "It's not like I'm not happy about it. But do you think we'll be ready that soon. Nothing's been set."

Danny spoke before the fire in Benjamin's eyes could rage into a torrent of ridiculous offending words. "What specifically concerns you Harris?"

"A few things."

"Such as?"

"First, how can they sign and promote us when we have no name? Secondly, we haven't found a style to market and appeal to anyone's appetite. I mean seriously, we're hard and heavy rockers, I hope, and Conner here looks like a timid John Mayer and Benjamin's standing over there with some Tyson Ritter-looking fucker who I have never heard of and have no idea what he's doing here. And thirdly, we have no original songs to brand us and a venue like Exit/In sort of calls for that. And lastly, I think more than what six, seven days of real practice might not be enough time to accomplish all of that."

Benjamin exploded, "Since when did you become all serious and knowing?"

Danny spoke firmly, "Benjamin! Back up. He was talking to me." Danny moved forward and sat on the step that led to the sunken den. "I am glad you are worried enough to point those things out Harris. It shows you are more than a party man. I read you all wrong….."

"Danny!"

She looked to Benjamin. "Grow up and shut up and pretend you care as much as he does. You should know these things as well. Danny looked at each of the band mates, "All of you listen. I am your manager.

Period! The buck starts and stops with me. Harris, Conner, Jay if you have questions or ideas bring 'em to me. Harris, you know the band scene, the talent, the players... I know the owners and the producers. I know promotion. Trust me. I have it all planned. You have a name, and I'll tell what it is when it's time. All of you separately and as a group will be spending time with a stylist and a photographer on Monday. I want you to know that I take all of you very seriously." She looked around at the handsome faces. Then focused in on Benjamin. "So Benjamin, why don't you introduce Jay to Harris and Conner and the other way round. And let them in on some of the songs we have."

"We?

"Benjamin, play nice."

"Guys, this is Jay. Danny brought him in to give us a more rounded sound. He'll play second lead and when needed rhythm lead, he'll also lend his vocals to back up when we need it for harmony."

Conner stepped forward to Jay and extended his hand. "Hey Jay, name's Conner and that crazy man with the bifocals is Harris."

"Good to meet you both. And may I say you're way too short to be John Mayer."

"Thanks Jay."

Benjamin looked to Conner and Jay, "If you're done with your bonding etiquette I want to assure all of you that the original content I bring to the table is good. it's solid, so from that angle we are covered."

Harris found an overwhelming urge to knock the overall condescending attitude right out of Benjamin. "Says the man who got upstaged by me and a last minute Britney Spears cover. Seriously?"

"Those were our over rehearsed songs we played that night. I have some songs that with a little work could be great. The other guys lacked the fire to make 'em work."

"The other guys lacked fire? What the fuck?" said Harris in a disgusted tone.

Benjamin looked at Harris, "It is possible to over rehearse. It is possible to get too comfortable to want to try new things."

Harris glared at Benjamin, he knew the truth, he had found out everything from Locker and the actual band mates that had walked out on Benjamin. And for the life of him, he just couldn't let it go. "I guess it's possible to get bored with the bullshit… where are these songs of fire? Cause I sure as shit ain't playing anything as weak as you played the other night."

"Weak? Those songs sure as hell were not weak!"

"Please, it was like giving the Backstreet Boys instruments and saying, "Go become a rock band."

"You four-eyed freak……."

Danny downed what was left of her drink and threw the glass across the room where it exploded against the massive fieldstone fireplace. Everyone looked at her. She allowed the sudden silence to become deafening. Taking a deep breath she intentionally yelled, "Will you tiny tots shut the fucking hell up!" Intentionally and with great forced control, she dropped her voice down to an octave above a whisper. "You are ruining my kick ass buzz. And I am beginning to think both of you could ruin a killer wet dream." Baring her teeth, raising her voice one more octave she carefully and slowly said; "Benjamin, give Harris the mother fucking songbook."

"But…"

"Now!" she hissed.

The room watched and waited in stunned silence as Benjamin stepped to the coffee table and picked up, then handed a Mead notebook to Harris. While everyone watched in frozen silence Harris began to flip through the pages.

Slowly and deliberately Danny stood up, readying herself to pounce if need be.

Harris broke the silence, "I like this one, if you part ways with the 'oh please watch as I slit my wrists in the middle of hot topic' vice of it all."

Benjamin looked at him. His eyes hard as glass. "What the fuck," he seethed.

"It's not all bad Benji. I can work with it; get the kinks out of it. Or better yet, get the real *Kinks* into it."

"What are you saying? It's a fucking masterpiece."

"It's an outline to a masterpiece."

Benjamin's heart beat wildly in his chest as he looked from Danny to Harris.

Harris rushed on with his critique. "Right now it's a bit too much poetry and not enough ball-grabbing rock."

Quickly, Danny forced herself to be sunny in an effort to calm the scene playing out in front of her. "Great. Now, how about you guys finish setting up and get to work on that?"

As if he hadn't heard her, Benjamin said to Harris; "If you are so all fucking knowing, where's your work?"

"No one asked me to bring it. But I got umpteen of these little spirals filled with words and even musical notes."

Benjamin yanked his notebook from Harris' hands. Turning on his heels, he strode to Danny and slammed the notebook into Danny's chest. He hissed though clenched teeth; "These are perfect." Looking into his eyes, she saw fear and more anger than she ever thought was possible for him to keep in. She refused to allow her gaze to follow him as he stormed from the room.

Quietly, she stepped down and toward Harris. She handed him the notebook. "For the record, you were right. I am impressed; you are the first person to have the balls to stand up to him and tell him like it is."

"Thank you."

"I will be back. You two listen to him and help him with what he has in mind." Danny turned and started from the room. She stopped at the doorway and turned around. "No one leaves. And if for any reason y'all ain't here when I get back, I will hunt you down and I will find you. Make no mistake, I will destroy you."

******

Danny stormed through the kitchen startling her assistant who was preparing the snack trays. Holding her hand up, she silenced the other woman before she could speak and continued onward to the back bedroom. She pushed the door open with such force that it crashed into the wall behind it. Once inside the room, she grabbed the heavy door and slammed it with such force that the house shook.

"Just what the motherfucking hell was that?"

Benjamin looked at her, he did not pretend to hide his hurt, and he matched her anger with pure hatred.

"I am done! Do you hear me? I am done with you and your 'management' style!"

Danny looked at him. Taking a deep breath, she matched his hate with stone cold indifference--an indifference that she channeled into pure unadulterated rage. She hissed, "Who the fucking hell do you think you are?"

"No, Bitch. The question is who the hell do you think you are?"

"I am the bitch who has bankrolled your sorry ass for I can't remember how many years. I am the sorry bitch who has stood behind you when I should've ran….."

"Ohhh…… let's bow down and pity little you."

She stepped forward and slapped him hard-- so hard he stepped back. Reflex brought his fist up. "Go ahead you little freak. Do it and die," she whispered in a tone of pure hatred. Backing up she continued, "You have a choice to make right now and I'll give you an hour to make it and follow through."

"Oh, you're giving me a choice?"

"Yes, I am."

"Who do you think…."

"I am the woman who owns your sorry ass and you best not forget that." She walked to the door, and turned and looked across the room with disgust. "You can either throw everything you wanted away and get the hell out of my house and out of my life or you can take a walk, breath, smoke a pack and grow a set and walk out there like a man, apologize and do your part to make your dream happen."

"Those are my fucking songs he wants to destroy."

"They will still be your songs. Only they will be marketable."

"But he….."

"You really don't know anything about your Harris Tweed do you? Well, I checked into him. He may be young and he may be crude but has two PhD's in music and writing. And a Masters in business. The man is literally a fucking genius."

She turned and started from the room.

"Do you know why I wanted him?"

"Yeah, and now you know why you need him."

Nick, a dark haired nonspecific Mediterranean man of about twenty-five enters the room from the attached bathroom. His rock hard body was unclothed. "Why do you guys have to fight in my fucking room?" He looked to the wall behind the door and noticed a hole the knob had made. "And why the fuck did you have to break my fucking wall?"

Danny looked at him. "Ain't nothing you can't fix Muffin Mix."

"Fuck!" he turned and went back into the bathroom.

Danny smiled, and then she took three steps toward Benjamin. Very softly, turning on all of her charm she said sweetly, "I hope you decide to get your act together and let those guys out there make you look as great as you are. Because in the end, it's all about the guy standing at the front center stage. And that is you."

Benjamin looked at her long and hard then he walked past her and slammed the door behind him.

Danny fell back on the bed and sunk down into the feather mattress. The blankets and pillows all but covered her.

Hearing the silence, Nick peeked his head out of the bathroom. Looking around he saw no one and a closed door. Thinking it was safe, he re-entered the room. Danny opened her eyes and saw Nick's manhood just above her. She sat straight up scaring him two steps backward.

"Jesus Christ! Danny!"

Danny picked up two pillows as she leapt to her feet. "For the love of God, Nick! Cover that thing up!" She threw the pillows at him as she spoke moving to the door. She stormed from the room.

Nick looked around him confused as he whispered, "But it's my room."

******

Benjamin's curiosity got the better of him, but his anger is what fueled him forward toward the den where the others were gathered. He reached the arched entry and stopped. He took several deep breaths in an effort to compose himself before entering the room. He rotated his head a few times forcing his neck to pop.

Harris looked over at Benjamin, "Just because I'm color blind doesn't mean I can't see shadows,"

Benjamin looked at Harris. Exhaling he stepped forward into the room. Harris extended his hand. "I didn't mean to be such a dick a second ago. But this here has to be a partnership between all of us; otherwise we're fucked before we even start. So, are you ready to listen for a minute and see what we can work out?"

Benjamin dropped Harris's hand and forced control into his voice. "Yeah, I'll listen. I just can't promise I'll like what I hear."

"Shit man. You are too serious. I'm going to be the one saying it, and I ain't even gonna make that promise."

Benjamin, set in his cocky anger, couldn't help but to give in to a smile.

Harris turned; he walked toward the others and picked up Benjamin's songbook as he talked. "So we three agree the gig coming up is cool but.... When we play we gotta play it quick. We're not going to have time to practice or do much composing. So, we three were thinking of a *Ramones* blitz type set. Four songs and we are off. We play 'em fast and straight through and get off the stage before anyone has a chance to realize that we suck. Cause we're gonna suck. Period. No way around it."

Benjamin's unexpected silence forced Harris to look up from the songbook to make sure he was still in the room. Benjamin returned his stare. "Okay... and?"

"Alright, so I haven't looked too deep at these lyrics, but one thing right now I see is that we can't do all these verses, choruses and repeats and changes. If we do the crowd'll realize we can't play shit one song in. So, out of all these, what's your favorite three?"

Benjamin took the songbook from Harris and thumbed through the pages. "Okay, here's one I like a lot... 'Katie Kutthroat'."

He handed the notebook back to Harris who took it and scanned quickly over it, "I like it." He ripped the page from the notebook.

"What the hell?" Benjamin lunged forward as Danny stepped in front of him. Benjamin continued to watch Harris who folded the page in half licked the crease and then tore the page in half.

"Okay. Now we have our first two songs to work with."

"Hey ass wipe! That was one song! Tearing the page in half doesn't make it two."

"You're right, it doesn't. You made it two songs when you added the second verse. Check it out. Throw in a chorus and it's a whole new ballgame."

Benjamin looked at Harris blankly as Harris handed him the two pieces of paper and turned back to the room where the others stood around with the instruments.

"Okay, Guys here's how it's gonna work. We're playin' fast and dirty like a blow job from an Asian crack whore. Benjamin, you'll start at the bottom half of the page, right after the part about the break up. Fifteen to twenty seconds on each verse and keep it at an even twenty on the choruses. The rest of us here will come in at an even three."

Harris moved and sat behind his drum set. Nervously, he tightened his hi-hat and looked to Conner. "You follow me in and give me something low and mid speed. Then keep the beat fast 'cause I'll be playing off you." He looked over to Jay, "When Conner finishes with the sex, we'll need you to slide, then keep it to three chords. Fiction, just scream this shit, jump in when it feels right and do your worst."

Harris hit out a roll on his floor tom, giving a nod to Conner, and before he ended the roll, the first play through of the song was off. And a band was born.

******

Danny stood just outside the den with a glass of bourbon in her hand. She liked what she was hearing. Two hours in, and they played like the true professionals they were meant to be. Smiling, she walked over to a table in the hall by the staircase. Biting her lip, she picked up the phone and dialed a number. There was an answer on the third ring.

"Hello, Gina Marie. Can you still make that opening at the studio happen tomorrow morning?"

"Yeah. So what happened? Did Benjamin kiss some ass and get his band back?"

Not quite. But we put something new together, and they're looking and sounding like it just might work out for the best."

"Well, I say record this puppy before it gets too long in the tooth. Consider it set."

"Thanks sugar. See you tomorrow."

Danny replaced the phone before Gina Marie could say good bye. She smiled wider and headed toward the kitchen to find Sarah, her assistant.

CHAPTER FIVE

Danny stood in the den's archway. She watched the sun stretch its rays across the bodies scattered about the room. Jay was stretched out in a chair that was propped against the wall at a tilt. Benjamin was stretched out in a recliner and Conner across a sofa. Danny took a gulp of her coffee-laced bourbon and smiled wickedly as she sat it down on a table next to the den's entrance. She had pink t-shirts slung over her shoulder. She stepped forward and looked down at Jay with a smile and kicked out the legs of his chair causing him to hit the floor. The sound of his crash to the hardwood woke up Benjamin and Conner who sat up looking around like confused prairie dogs.

"Rise and shine my pretty darlings!"

Jay looked up at her from the floor, "What the fuck do you think you are doing, bitch?!"

"Don't whine Jay, you are not livestock."

Rubbing the sleep from his eyes, Benjamin looked at her, "What's up, Babe? Couldn't you let us sleep?"

"I let ya'll sleep as long as I could. Any longer and we'll be late for the studio."

Conner flipped his recliner forward and sat straight up. "Studio? How long was I out?" He looked around him as if to confirm where he was. "What did I miss?"

"Danny, Babe. We're not ready for a studio yet," Benjamin said putting his feet onto the floor.

Danny tossed out the t-shirts. "My ears say otherwise. Plus, this is the only time I could get us in our price point. So unless *Fictional Silence* is getting back together, *The Velvet Clutches* are going to have to do it."

Conner looked at the shirt still dazed, "Who are they?"

"All those lying before me in my den."

Jay looked around him. He still sat on the floor where he had been dumped. "Where's Harris? Did he quit?"

Benjamin looked up from the shirt in his hand to Danny, "Who gave you naming rights?"

"I took the rights very early this morning when Sarah and I started screening those beauties."

As Danny talked, Harris walked into the room dressed in his t-shirt and a pair of boxers. Benjamin looked at him, "Why are you half-dressed?"

Danny chimed. "Where'd you get that shirt?"

Harris put up his hands and smiled. "Slow down, gear it back a notch... The blood hasn't gotten all the way back to my small head yet."

Conner laughed.

Jay said, "Nice one."

Harris smiled and looked toward Benjamin and Danny, "The chick I boned in the laundry room, gave it to me since she ripped my other one. Pretty cool, huh? Don't know who they are, but I'll check 'em out on MySpace later."

Smiling, Benjamin shook his head, "Good luck, I doubt they have a page yet."

Danny, appalled and recovering, peeped, "You fucked Sarah? My Sarah?" Danny wheeled around and took in all those in the room, "Mouths shut when you see Nick! All of you! Mouths shut when you meet Nick!" Danny stepped up nose-to-nose with Harris and said, "Never, ever touch Sarah again! Never! You got that?"

"Yes ma'am!" Harris croaked.

Danny started to walk from the room yelling as she left, "All of ya'll get ready. Now! Matt Brown will be here any minute with the van." She muttered under her breath as she left the room.

Benjamin got to his feet. "We gotta clean up and wake up. Ya'll know where the bathrooms are." Benjamin left the room and ran up the stairs.

Harris looked around at Conner and Jay, "So, where are we going in such a rush?"

"Apparently *The Velvet Clutches* are recording today." Conner mumbled as he walked from the room.

Harris answered his explanation with a, "And?"

"We are *The Velvet Clutches*." Conner called from the doorway as he kept walking.

"Cool." Harris turned to Jay; you know velvet clutches is a Japanese euphemism for 'pussy'?"

"We're not ready for a show in seven days and yet you are cool with us recording today?"

"Dude, recording studios have free food and I'm broke as hell and down about thirteen thousand calories from fucking while standing for three hours. It's harder to do than you think... So I'm all for a free meal."

Jay shook his head, "Dude, put some pants on because you're free balling it right now."

Looking down Harris said. "Yeah.Well," adjusting his boxers he continued, "If you were a shrub underneath a tree this huge you'd be taking every chance you had to get some air too." Harris walked over to where his pants lay.

"How?.... What?...." A puzzled Jay looked away from Harris and saw Sarah, a beautiful blue eyed china doll leaning in the doorway smiling coyly at Harris.

She turned her head and called out, "Hey, Nick, hurry it up, I'm starving."

She made an about face and marched back down the hallway.

Jay looked at Harris. "Was that, *the* Sarah?"

Harris just smiled and nodded as he zipped his jeans.

******

Danny stood on her front porch next to the open doors. A tall, lanky, long haired young man no older than eighteen stood beside her.

"So Matt, you remembered the case of Red Bull?"

"Yes ma'am. It's in the van."

"Everything loaded?"

"Everything 'cept the bodies."

"You go take out a four-pack of the Red Bull and put it in my car and I'll get the bodies loaded."

"Sure thing Miss Danny."

Matt B. ran off to a clean white Econo-line van and pulled open the back doors. Danny turned back to the house, "Come on guys, Move it! Move it!"

Conner and Harris ran past her. "Benjamin, hurry up! We're gonna be late!"

Benjamin yelled back, "Give me another minute!"

"Jesus!" Danny muttered just as Jay was approaching. "Someone remind me never to date a guy who takes longer than I do to get ready."

Jay stopped, "Hey Danny, never date a guy who takes longer than you do to get ready."

"Shut your smart mouth and get that smart ass in the van."

"Whatever." Jay laughed and ran down the steps.

Harris looked at Jay, "The love birds getting catty?"

"Get your ass in the van, Tweed!"

Harris smiled, turned and took a running leap onto Jay's back causing both of them to fall into the van through the side door. Danny, smiling at the antics called out, "Are you guys kids or adults?"

All the guys began to laugh.

Benjamin blew past Danny and jumped into the convertible without opening the door. He blew the horn and called, "Hurry it up Danny! Time's a wasting."

******

Conner was the last by several minutes to enter the front doors of The Bomb Shelter Studios with his bass slung over his shoulder. He looked lost and confused by his surroundings as he approached the most beautiful woman he had ever laid eyes on, Gina Marie, who was going through papers at the front desk.

She looked up at him and was instantly lost in his sea green eyes. "Can I help you with anything, Honey?"

"I kind of got ditched in the parking lot. I'm supposed to be recording with Benjamin and everyone else today."

"Ah… Would have never guessed it. You look too sweet and innocent to be one of Danny's boys."

"I… I don't know if I could be called one of her boys or not."

"Trust me, you're here, you're one of hers. For better or worse."

"I expect to keep it for the better."

"Well, aren't you a treasure! Come on, Hon and follow me. I'll take you to 'em."

******

Conner walked into a very sizeable room with posh furniture and a state of the art sound board that had Danny sitting behind it. "Where's Gina?" She asked.

"She had to take a call."

"So what do you think?"

"It's not at all what I expected. Yet, it's more than I could've dreamed of."

"Well, I like to think of it as Music City's Abby Road."

"Who is Gina?"

"My best and closest spirit sister. Do I need to warn her that yet another rock star is smitten by her charms?"

"Does she have something against rock?"

"She is a country girl in every way there is to be country."

"Well then I'd much appreciate it if there's nothing said 'bout me either way."

"Gotcha," Danny turned and looked in the booth window. Harris was jumping and appeared to be screaming. He waved his hands around pointed to Conner. He was oblivious to the fact that he was not making a sound to the outside world. Danny smiled, "I think you're wanted inside."

"It looks that way." Conner nods to her and heads inside the booth.

Conner, no sooner opened the door, than Harris started ranting in pure childlike excitement. "Dude! How fucking cool is this? The fridge out there is packed with imports and I mean premium shit. And Danny just got Manny's House to bake us some pies before they even open up. She is definitely a fucking goddess. She's gonna have that skinny boy go pick 'em up in a few....."

"Hey! Earth to Fat Boy. This skinny boy has a name: It's Matt B."

"Whatever. You're still a skinny boy. Just think, Conner how cool it's gonna be. Cold beer and warm pizza for breakfast. It's usually the other way around."

Conner just smiled, "That is pretty tight."

From the back of the room , Benjamin called out, "How about you two carry on the conversation while Conner plugs in. I mean we only have today to get whatever we're doing here done."

Danny's voice chimed in from the control booth, "You mean you only have a few hours, don't you Hun?"

"No Babe. We have all day. I checked Gina's schedule before I came back here. I texted Ben of *The Comfies* and traded a Friday headliner at The Muse for them not to come today."

"Crafty of you."

Benjamin gave her a mischievous smile.

Gina Marie entered the control room and her voice carried over the speaker to the guys, "Hey Danny, I have great news. *The Comfies* rescheduled so today is all yours."

Clapping and cheering came from the recording booth.

"Mattie B, it's time for you to leave these degenerates and grab me a carton of smokes when you pick up the pies."

"I'm on it, Miss Danny." He walked out of the room.

Danny spoke once more into the mic, "Are you boys ready to play?" They all nodded. "Tell me what order you're going in with the music."

"Just like the last set we ran through last night," Benjamin replied.

Harris spoke up, "Except we're running each song twice and recording you two and myself as the instrumentals only for the overlay."

Jay replied, "Sounds sweet."

"Hey Babe?"

"What do you need Benjamin?"

"You will have my vocals cranked, right?"

"Yes sweetie. I got you running three notches above everyone else."

"That's cool."

Conner spoke up, "Are we gonna talk or are we gonna play?"

Harris grinned, "Let's lay it down like a Milf."

******

Later that evening, Gina Marie and Danny sat at Gina's kitchen table. A laptop sat between them with music blasting from it. Gina reached out and turned the volume down, "It's not bad for a day's work. Actually, it's quite exceptional. To be honest, we have bands in and out of the studio every day and only a handful are lucky enough to put something this good together in a few months of work. Yet, of course, none of them have a sound engineer who has been honing her skills since before she could walk."

"Oh please. You are far too kind, considering you've been doing the same for as long as I have, and you are probably better at it than I am."

"Oh, Lady Bug, I will not fight that statement coming from you of little praise."

"Seriously. Do you think you can find someone to press out at least a hundred of it by show time?"

"We both know who has to be asked, and you know you could ask just as easily as me."

"Please Gina. I really don't wanna walk back across that bridge."

"Hon, you know it wasn't his fault and one day you're gonna have to get over it."

"But I really can't have that someday be right now."

Gina considered her friend. After a long pause she replied, "Okay, but this is the last time. Do you have the designs for the cover art?"

"I have Sarah working on it. She should be done tomorrow. I'll e-mail it as soon as I have it."

"You are lucky I'm gonna to tell him it's for you. Otherwise a four-day turn around on any order at all would get me thrown out of his shop for life."

"Okay. I get it. I'll send him a thank you card with a bottle and break the ice. I'm gonna change the subject now."

"No more business?"

"All done on that front. It's girl time. I think you made a good impression on one of my boys."

"Oh, please. A boy is not what I need right now."

"Come on! I haven't see you with a guy in over a year."

"And with good reason. Besides, who says I'm not happy just the way things are?"

"Oh and who told me not twenty seconds ago that I was the one who needed to get over things?"

"Well let's see. I said I'd never date another musician again, especially a rocker. So if I'm gonna be true to my own self-promises, and since I work only with rock musicians fourteen hours a day, seven days a week trying to keep the studio going, I don't see a dating life in sight. Unless, of course, you know, I could date the 60-year-old UPS guy. Or how about Chang?"

"Who is Chang?"

"He's the little Chinese guy that delivers my sesame chicken every day. He's probably 70."

"My, my, my."

"Listen, Danny I appreciate your concern. But my life is fine. The only guys I meet, who aren't still hot for their exes, are just bunches of overgrown boys or overly pompous jerks trying to slice out a nearly impossible dream with marginal talent and egos as fragile as rice paper. And all the time they're pretending they're getting somewhere, life is passing them by."

"My, oh my, aren't you little Miss Cynical."

"Nope, just honest."

"Aren't you in the least bit curious about which one it is that's so hot for you?"

"I can probably guess. Let's see; we know it ain't Benjamin. So I'm gonna guess that it's not gonna be either the sexual harassment lawsuit waiting to happen Buddy Holly looking one or the I'm so cool because I don't care dick about any female."

Danny began to laugh and did so hard that tears spilled down her cheeks. "How the hell did you know that Jay didn't? …"

"To quote my Daddy, "That man is too Rock Hudson to ever be confused with John Wayne."

Both girls laughed until their sides ached, and their cheeks hurt. Finally, between huge gulps of air Danny said, "No. Seriously, it ain't Harris, it's Conner."

"The short bass player who wore the Cheap Trick shirt?"

"You see you already have a common musical interest."

"Oh yeah… like I'm going to rush head long into a new relationship with a guy based on my unhealthy liking of Cheap Trick."

"Means he's a closet country boy."

"Maybe. But there's no guarantee."

"You'll never know till you ask."

"How about we change the subject?"

"How about we find a movie? I've got the big liquor-sneaking purse."

"Sneaking liquor into a movie? When did we go back to high school?"

"Some things you just never outgrow."

"Let me change shirts and get my keys, 'cause I assume I'll be the only one able to drive by the closing credits."

"You know me too well!"

CHAPTER SIX

666

It was the big night. The debut of *The Velvet Clutches* was only a few hours away. Conner, Harris and Jay sat around a grimy table backstage. Lines of coke were in front of them.

Harris raised his head from the table, "I honestly don't think my balls will ever forgive me for wearing these pants."

Jay took the rolled up dollar from Harris' hand, "Suck it up bitch. It's part of the style."

"Personally Jay, my man, I don't see how Benjamin has anything left hard enough to fuck the Nazi bitch. It's gonna take at least a day before I'm ready to go. And all she had me do was wear these pants."

"Hey guys, she's not all that bad."

"What you don't understand, Conner is that an actual label couldn't push out this much shit this fast. You know how long it took my former band to pick a name? Three months. It was almost a year before our first show."

Jay set his beer bottle at his feet, "Weren't you in a cover band?"

"Per say... We may have covered songs, but we rewrote and tweaked them to make 'em better."

"Conner sipped his beer, "I can believe that. Granted, I only know what you did with Benjamin's songs."

"Shit, Conner, it was a hell of a lot easier with Benjamin's shit. If this thing works out even in a minor sort of way, we've got eight albums in that notebook of his. He'd be a dangerous motherfucker if he could compose worth a shit and wasn't so damned insecure."

Conner laughed, "Well, he's got you now man; start teaching."

Harris snorted another line. "Shit... I'm not one to do teaching, I can't read music worth shit. Most of what I learned, I learned by ear. I just know what sounds good, plays through. I hate hiccups, repeats, and stilts."

Jay took the dollar from Harris, "I learned from my dad. He had this band in L.A, *The Outlaw Lovers*. They were pretty good until he started losing control, you know...givin' in to his vices. Then, it suddenly became about makin' me a star. He had me playing in bands with 30- year-old guys in dives and shit holes by the time I was 12. I split when I was 17. Tried Austin for a few years. Boring. Too much going on there, the whole indie scene. Heard there was a rock uprisin' here, 'cause there wasn't enough country to go around. So, here I am."

Harris looked over, "So, how 'bout you Conner, my boy? What's your story?"

"Took lessons, fell in love with Cheap Trick. Then stumbled into Southern Rock. *Molly Hatchet, ZZ Top, Better Than Ezra*, and so on. Saw the roots of what they did in old Country before this current trend of pop infused country shit. Came here with visions of startin' my own genre. Got here and found it's not so easy. So, now I sleep on your stained mattress in your hall closet and I play in some rock band with guys I barely know and horror of horrors, I am having to learn to walk, sit and even stand in jeans that are two sizes too tight."

Harris laughed, "Fucking sucks to be you, huh? Hey you wanna bump a line or no?"

"It's not really my thing, man."

Jay laughed.

"Cool. But FYI, I've done it a million times. It ain't gonna kill... Well, there's a better than average chance you are not gonna die from it." He extends the rolled up dollar to Conner. "Your choice, bro. No hard feelings."

Conner looked at him for several long seconds. Then reached out and took the dollar. Hesitantly, he snorted a quarter line before jumping up from the table. "Fuck that burns like hell."

Harris and Jay burst out laughing.

Harris was the first to speak up, "We all say that the first time, Man. If you don't want any more, cool beans, Benjamin will lap it up." Harris leaned over and opened a small cooler at his side. "Here man, have a beer."

Conner stepped forward, after taking the beer he sat down. "Thanks man."

"No prob... Hey... Oh shit! Did I tell you what I did this morning?"

Jay shook his head, "I don't wanna know. No disrespect man but I've only known you three days and I already know too much about who and what you've done and did."

Harris laughed. "Get your mind out of the fucking gutter. So, anyway, I know the guy who does the flyers and shit for the Exit/In." He reached into his hip pocket and took out a folded piece of paper and tossed it on the table in front of Jay. "Check that shit out."

Conner grabbed the paper and unfolded it. "Wow! The question is does Feeble Weiner know we're now closing the show?"

Jay grabbed the paper. "What?! Hellz yeah! This is fucking cool."

Harris looked at Jay. "What the fuck dude?"

"What'd I do?"

"Hellz yeah?... What the hell, Bro. Hell with a z? You ain't black. Stop pretending man. You are white and you look nothing like Marky Mark or any other member of the Funky Bunch." Harris started laughing.

"What now?" Jay asked, barely concealing his anger.

"If I was blind, I might think you were the founding member of that Funky Bunch since you started wearing that new cologne."

Jay flipped Harris the bird as Benjamin came through the door.

Conner looked at Harris, "You know, dude, you had a pretty good burn going until you threw in Marky and the Funky Shit."

"Yeah, man, that made it sound like you were trying too hard," added Jay.

"Fuck you both dudes. You sir, Conner my boy, can sleep in the yard tonight for all I care." Harris turned to Benjamin. "Save the night man and snort the rest of this shit."

"No thanks dude. I'm playing it straight."

"You traitorous pussy!" Harris said, in mock slander.

"Drunken ass wrangler." Benjamin retorted.

"And just how is that an insult?"

Benjamin reached out and picked up the flyer, "What's this for?"

"A flyer for a show," said Jay draining his beer.

Benjamin scanned it, "What the fuck? We're not headlining?"

"Ahhh, but it takes a trained eye to realize that." Harris said in a calming manner hoping to talk to Benjamin from the angry place he was heading.

"We can't let them use this." Benjamin said hitting a paper.

"It's too late." Harris said taking the flyer from him refolding it as he continued, "This is the final print, it's already posted. Don't worry. It can't do your rep too bad to close."

"You, Harris, are an asshole."

Harris painfully put the paper back into his pocket, "And you, sir, are a first-rate cunt."

"Dick."

"I won't argue with that one."

Jay and Conner laughed.

Benjamin said, "Give me the damn bill, I need a bump now."

******

Benjamin, Jay and Danny stood together at the stage end of the bar at the Exit/In. Jay and Danny were working to calm a Benjamin who was awash with stage jitters turning to rage.

"Seriously! We go on in twenty minutes! Where the fuck are they?!"

Danny kept her voice calm yet stern. "Would you just chill. You know Harris. He'll be here with Conner any minute."

"What about set up?"

"Honey. Think. This is a plug and play venue. They use a house drum kit. All Harris has to do is bring his sticks."

Jay offered Benjamin a shot glass, "Take a shot; it'll relax you."

"Fuck no! Are you crazy? Never before a show."

Jay shrugged and knocked back the shot himself as Conner with Gina Marie by his side walked up to them.

"Hey guys, how's……"

Benjamin snapped, "Where the hell is Harris?!"

"I don't know. I caught a ride over with Gina Marie."

Danny couldn't help but to smile. "So you two came together?"

Gina Marie looked at Danny shaking her head. "It's not like that at all. We both ended up at Spring Water, and I didn't think Conner should have to walk."

Benjamin looked from Gina Marie to Conner. "And just how did you get to Spring Water?"

"Harris' dad dropped me off over on West End to explore while he and Harris went into Bellevue to see his grandmother."

"Well, where's your bass?"

"With Harris. I mean I wasn't going to carry it around with me all afternoon."

"Oh great. Just fucking great. We have no rhythm section. None. Nada. Fucking zippola."

Conner replied, "Relax ,man. Harris is too hyped about tonight to stand us up."

Gina Marie placed her hand on Conner's shoulder, "Yeah Benjamin. Conner's right. There's plenty of time yet."

Benjamin looked at Gina Marie as if she had gone mad, "Great, just fucking great. A fantastic night like this wouldn't be complete without little Ms. Bitch chiming in."

Danny stepped in between Gina Marie and Conner and Benjamin. "Benjamin!" Looking into his eyes so he could be sure to see the fire in her own. "You apologize and walk away or else…"

"Or else what, Ice Queen?"

Conner and Jay looked at each other and nodded. Jay stepped forward and put a hand on Benjamin's shoulder and turned him around. "Let's go, get plugged in."

Conner followed Jay and Benjamin toward the stage. Danny looked back to Gina Marie. "I'm so sorry. He's just on edge."

"Don't worry. He'd only bother me if I bothered to pay attention to him."

"Sometimes Gina, sometimes I hate him so much that…"

Gina Marie reached out and put her hand on Danny's shoulder. "For the life of me, I'll never understand the 'sometimes' in that sentence. But it's your life. So, I have the presses in my car. They came out fantastic. One thing though, Stacy said he was coming to see if your boys are really that good or if all the buzz was just your PR skills."

"Oh fuck! Why?"

"It's not a private show Danny. The man can come if he wants. I don't think Benjamin would be that stupid."

"Let's hope not… Where are you parked?"

"Right next to you around back."

"Good, we'll get that bouncer Willie to help us with the stuff. I got the t-shirts and posters in my car."

******

Jay and Conner stood in front of Benjamin as he leaned in a corner just below the back of the stage smoking a cigarette.

Jay was trying to talk Benjamin down from his rage and jitters. "Dude you gotta be relaxed before you head on stage. Otherwise you will make mistakes. Trust me, this I know."

"Fuck you. We're 10 minutes away from looking like first-class assholes."

No one had seen him walk up. So when he spoke, "Bad news dude. No matter what your momma said, you already look like an asshole." They all wheeled around and looked at Harris as if they had seen a ghost. "So what's up with the standing in a corner thing? Are you getting ready to start a corn holin' chain? Cause if you are maybe we should change our name to something like Harris Tweed and the three fags."

Benjamin leaped forward when his shocked paralysis had broken its hold on him. "Where the hell have you been?"

"Standing over in that corner," he pointed, "talking to those two girls," he waved and they waved back. "Before that I was at my grandma's."

"You are late! You do know that don't you?"

"Nope. I got here a good hour before you and a good two hours before Conner," he looked to Conner, "And I must say good for you, she's hot as all hell."

"Thanks."

Benjamin spat out, "No you haven't. I've been watching the door for an hour at least."

Harris smiled. He truly relished Benjamin's near hysteria. "Bro, look over in that corner where I was talking to the babe. See those two big doors on the left side of the sandy blonde with the huge knockers. You should've looked that way. I've been going in and out of those for the last couple of hours."

Jay made an attempt to lighten the growing anger and spoke smiling, "I'll sure be watching those double D's for the rest of tonight."

"I meant the doors Jay, not the tits, but yet, of course, now that we got this settled... Not a bad idea. Why don't you guys go plug in and tune up I'm gonna go shot gun a beer and a whiskey double, then I'll meet you up there and we'll get this show thing going."

"My bass up there?"

"It sure is. I hid it behind the drums – wouldn't want that serious ride to do a fast and furious."

Harris walked off toward the bar as Conner leapt to the stage. Benjamin looked at Jay, "What the hell is wrong with Harris?"

"It's not him you should be asking that question about."

******

The lights on the stage lowered. Conner, Jay and Benjamin stood huddled in front of Harris, who whispered, "OK, Remember, keep it fast. I'll set the line, Conner, after that it's up to you." Conner nodded to him. "Are we ready to do this?"

Jay looked at Benjamin, "Are you cool with the solos Benjamin or do you want me to go ahead and take 'em?"

"I've got 'em."

"OK, dudes, let's scream it straight through."

The guys broke and headed to their microphone stands. Harris smacked his sticks together, "One, two, fuck it through." He rolled the song and followed with a beat by Conner, a beat behind him Jay and Benjamin joined.

Midway through the first song, Benjamin blew his three-chord solo which caused him to lose his words for the briefest of moments. He recovered quickly. The first song faded seamlessly into the second which was played flawlessly. When it came time for another lead solo rift, Jay looked over to Benjamin as he jumped it and played it through before Benjamin could. Jay continued this trend through the next two songs. Conner walked a few extra chords at the end of the set and the crowd, who had been unaware of the tension and scene stealing on stage, erupted in a wild appreciation.

Benjamin jerked a plug from his guitar and sent it around to his back as he put his foot on the bass drum and pushed off of it to jump in the air almost tripping a whole drum kit back on Harris. He turned and within two strides he stood face-to-face with Jay who was unplugging.

"What the fuck man?!"

"You blew the first, Benjamin. I'm never gonna let you fuck a set just cause you can't chill and work it fast."

Jay turned and started off stage followed closely by Benjamin. Benjamin put his hand on Jay's shoulder and spun him around to face him. "We are not done yet."

"You have never been so right!"

Jay head butted Benjamin causing him to fall backwards onto the stage. Instantly blood spurted from his nose. The crowd erupted again as Conner rushed over pushing Jay back off the stage and Harris helped Benjamin up from the stage.

******

Danny and Harris had ushered Benjamin out of the Exit/In. Once he was in the car with Danny, Harris went back to check on Gina Marie and give her updates on the change of plans there. He was on stage loading the guitars with Jay and Conner's help. He and Conner got Jay calmed then took him over to join up with Danny and Benjamin in the back room at The Gold Rush.

Danny had managed to get Benjamin cleaned up and his broken nose set. So there he was sitting at a table wearing a Gold Rush T-Shirt and nursing a large tumbler of bourbon when Harris, Conner and Jay walked in.

Danny looked up at them as they entered, "Instruments secured?"

"Yes ma'am." They all responded.

"Gina and Willie covering sales and inquiries for me?"

"Yes." Harris answered.

"Harris you sit next to Benjamin, Conner you sit next to Jay."

Jay sneered, "I wouldn't touch him if my life depended on it……"

"Touch me again and you got no life."

"Boys! Enough!" Danny looked from Benjamin to Jay. "This gets settled now!"

Benjamin looked up at her with fire in his eyes. "I don't have shit to settle with this, this thief!"

"Thief? You're the insecure narcissistic……"

"Boys!" Yelled Danny. "We settle this now."

"I got nothin' to settle. It's all his fault! It's all on him . He's a psycho!"

"Me? Fuck that shit! It's settled when you learn to play guitar."

"When I learn to play?"

"Yea, you!" Jay spat. "A professional band doesn't have time for some fear- ridden amateur to hunt for chords to play."

Danny exploded cutting Benjamin off before he could say anything, "Shut the fuck up right now! Both of you! Jay! I don't give a damn about your personal feelings. This is a business deal. I brought you into a fold and you were supposed to do as you were told." Danny turned on Benjamin. "And you! Benjamin! If you know you can't do something grow the fuck up. Be man enough to hand it off to someone who can until you learn it.

Despite whatever god mentality you have 'Fiction,' you are still limited by Benjamin. Because you are just Benjamin first. And you." Danny looked at Conner and Harris. "This is your band as well! I count on you two to end stuff like this before it happens."

"We didn't exactly kn……."

"Shut your smart ass mouth, Harris! I know damn well you are more perceptive than anyone in this room."

Benjamin slammed his fist on the table causing his glass to jump, "Will you shut the hell up! No one knew this fucker was a psycho! And this psycho fucker attacked me! This is my band! And I want him out and play this as a three piece."

"Your band?" Harris said with a bit of awe.

"Yeah you heard him right, Harris. He thinks it is all his and everyone is disposable."

"You are disposable!" Shouted Benjamin.

"All I did was make damn sure you didn't fuck the rest of us over with your arrogant inexperience. You know what? Fire my fucking ass! That's fucking fine with me! I don't wanna stay around and watch you destroy every chance you get and everyone you touch in an effort to feed your insecure arrogant, assholistic neurosis." Jay leapt to his feet and turned to Danny, "Fuck our deal bitch! You are just as neurotically insecure as he is and he'll destroy you just like he'll destroy himself. I'll be fine without your plan or your help. So fuck you and fuck him!" Jay slammed out of the room.

Benjamin turned on Danny, "Just what fucking plan was that pansy ass talking about?"

"It was nothing, that means even less now."

Harris stood abruptly, "OK, so we have some changes to make. I say tomorrow, for now you guys do whatever. I'm checkin' out for the night getting' shit faced, laid and eatin' my grandma's leftover tomato macaroni and cheese." He reached into his pocket and pulled out his keys and tossed them to Conner. "You, sir, can go wherever, whenever. I'll be in no shape to drive within the hour." Harris walked out with a wave.

Benjamin looked over at Conner, "So what do you have to say?"

"Shit happens."

"That's all you got?"

"Too much has already been said. Does anymore need to be said? What's said, what's done can't be unsaid or undone. So we'll face what's left tomorrow."

"I agree," Danny said. "We'll fix the hole tomorrow."

"Well ya'll, I promised Gina a drink so I'm headed out."

With those words Conner walked tiredly, somehow defeated, from the room.

"So……….."

Benjamin turned on Danny, "I can't believe you had a side deal with that ass."

"It was nothing."

"Whatever happened to 'everything I do is for you'?"

"The deal with him was designed to help you."

"Yeah sure, you fucking lied to me. You've always told me that everything is all about me."

"And you have fought me and self-destructed at every step. Like a fucking roller coaster in a fun house. Not once did it ever occur to you that maybe just once, I needed something, anything to be about me?"

"No. No it never did. Cause there's not one thing that could've been about you."

"Good God Benjamin! Where the fuck did you go?"

Stacy, a big man with a big presence entered the room.

"I hope I'm not interrupting anything important."

At the sound of his voice, Danny's spine straightened and she wheeled around, "As always, your timing is as impeccable as a heart attack on a wedding night."

"And you, Danny are as charming as always."

"What the hell do you want Stacy?"

"Relax, My Lady, it's not you I want. It's that man behind you."

"He's not interested. Get out!"

"Is this true? Does she speak for you Son?"

"Depends on the subject."

Stacy held up a CD, "How about the subject of pressing a thousand more of these and giving you guys 10 k bonus to join Spat Records?"

"That's something I could discuss."

"Good, then shall we?" Stacy motioned to the door.

"Benjamin don't." Danny hissed through clenched teeth. "You have to trust me on this. You don't want to do business with this guy."

Benjamin looked over and she could see he was in full self-destruct mode. "You should consider now, this, as your time. Because this is about me and doesn't concern you at all."

"But it does concern the others."

"I am the band."

Benjamin turned his eyes from her and began to move forward.

"Come Benjamin, let me buy you a beer."

Benjamin walked past Stacy and out the door.

"Benjamin! Don't!"

"You, Lady need to learn real fast that if you can't piss for distance, you shouldn't get into pissing matches with those born for the distance."

"I've seen the package, what birthright are you claiming?"

Stacy laughed and left the room.

"Damn you Benjamin." Danny whispered to the empty room.

******

Danny sat alone on her bed. An uncorked bottle of Rock Hill Bourbon was on her night stand. A mirror was in her hand and a line of coke called to her from its reflection. She snorted the line and laid the mirror next to the bourbon. She was leaning forward when Benjamin walked into the room.

"I see your night cap is still going strong."

"How was your beer with Stacy?"

"Okay. He has a lot of plans he wants to make official with contracts tomorrow."

"I hope you read the terms well. Pay attention to the punctuation that's where he likes to trap people."

"You have no faith in me."

"I have faith in you. Not him."

"Why don't you want me to be a success?"

"I've worked my ass off to make you a success. What I don't want is to see you become another Mondo Primo."

"Would that really be so bad?"

"Only if you don't mind being a moderately successful rock star, working as a houseboy for me in exchange for room, board and a little cash under the table having your girlfriend pay for everything, because Stacy took 90 percent of the money your band made when signed with a major label and the other 10 percent went to tour cost. No I'm sure Nick will tell you he enjoyed every second of knowing he has to make two more albums just to see any money for all his hard work."

"Stacy explained that."

"Oh really. And just what's his version of Nick's harsh reality?"

"He told me the way Nick wanted to release the EP ran up costs and that he had to recoup and that the money he's going to make from the next album will be the original cut promised to him in the contract."

"It's bullshit Benjamin! I read the contract when Nick asked for advice on it. I warned him; but in the end all he saw was the small chunk of upfront cash. In comparison, if he would've waited he'd be better off right now."

"How do you know? Huh? You forget, I'm not Nick. I'm smarter, more talented. This is my first real shot Danny. I have to take it."

Danny got up from the bed and walked toward him.

"Promise me you'll talk it over with Conner and Harris. Give 'em the pro's and con's. At least let me work out the contract with him. I know where his bones are buried."

"Danny, I'm a man...."

"Please Benjamin, I love you. In the end if you live with me, I want it to be because you want to not because you have to."

"Fine. But you have to promise me that you will get the deal done, 'cause I want this."

"I'll make it work. I promise."

"You ready for bed?"

"I'm always ready to share a bed with you."

CHAPTER SEVEN

777

It had been two weeks since the debut of *The Velvet Clutches*. The now trio had performed to sold out venues all over Nashville. Danny had worked nonstop soothing nerves, keeping people together, and she knew all her work including, negotiations with Stacy was going to be Benjamin's undoing. This was his longest self-destruct obsession that she had ever witnessed. It seemed that the more success and praise he reaped, the more determined he was to undermine it. The more venue requests, CD and souvenir sales that were made, the more Benjamin was convinced that Stacy could multiply it and of course, the more successful The Velvet Clutches, the more adamant Benjamin was that Stacy would represent them.

In an effort to undermine and appease Benjamin, Danny and Gina Marie had formed a company and offered Benjamin double Stacy's deal. Benjamin refused her "charitable" attempts at controlling him. Nick tried to talk to Benjamin but Benjamin just called him a loser.

Conner and Harris listened and even agreed with Danny, worried over Benjamin, who made it clear it was his or no way at all. Benjamin did as Harris said when it came to musical arrangements and song placement but business and where the band was headed – that was made clear that it was to be Benjamin's way or no way at all.

Danny would admit that she spent too much time with the J. Bourbon brothers: Jim, John, Jack and Jamison; but even the J. Brothers couldn't stop the pieces of Benjamin's true self from emerging into a neat and tidy picture before her eyes. And she knew that if he didn't do one of his complete turnarounds soon she'd be unable to hold it back and she knew…………………..

As she stood at the entrance to the den listening in on the tail end of his phone conversation, God help her. She knew that if the truth didn't turn him, she'd have to love him enough to lose him.

"Yeah man…. No problem……… sure, works for me," Benjamin turned and saw her entering the room. "Can we finish this later?……. Alright man, catch you later."

"Who was that?" Danny asked walking into the room.

"No one, just setting up a lunch with a friend."

Danny sat in a chair across from him. "Oh. I got some bad news for you Babe."

"Really. What's that?"

"As you know I've been working with Stacy trying to make a deal for you."

"Come on! Don't tell me you fucked that up for me."

"I've argued with him for two weeks now. He's refused to make even one concession."

"So? Maybe that's because his deal is good the way that it is. Did you ever think of that?"

"He's intent on screwing you over........."

"Come off it!" Benjamin said leaping to his feet.

"You need to wake the fuck up! The contract he's offering is identical to Nick's. I will not let him do this to you."

"Aren't you just being jealous?"

"Jealous?"

"Yeah. Maybe your ego is in the way."

"My ego?"

"Yeah. Your ego. You can't see that this is a great opportunity for me because you don't want to admit that he can do more for me than you can."

Despite her anger, Danny leaned back in her chair and laughed. "How do you figure that? When you know damn well that no one has done more for you than I have."

Benjamin turned on her, "You really think you have done so much for me? Then why the hell is it that I have followed your fucking "plan" for almost two years now and haven't gotten anywhere. No tours, no real money, nothing!"

Danny leapt to her feet. And stood nose- to-nose with Benjamin. "Following? Oh... Oh you mean fighting my plan."

"Fighting?"

"Yeah fighting against it all."

"And when …. name one time…."

"Why don't I just give you a list."

"You don't have a list. I dare you to come up with more than one thing……"

"You didn't feel the energy with your first band *Fuzz*. You broke up the second band *Dime Cheap* because your drummer wrote a song. Oh, and how about three weeks ago when you ended *Fictional Silence* because in your words here: "a half-ass drunken drum bum" upstaged you?"

Benjamin turned and stepped away from her. She continued on, "The truth is you can't stick with anything long enough to make it work for you! The minute a hint of success is in the air, you sabotage it. What is happening now is pure fucking timing and a hell of a lot of me doing what you should've been doing. I got the studio time. I got Jay to make you look better. I got those albums pressed. I got the bookings. I made the promotional souvenirs. I got the websites up and running. God help me, but it's even because of me that Stacy had the chance to hear you. This band you call yours….. This band is more me than you… I fucking named you for god's sake! You haven't done a damn thing that I have asked of you without hemming and hawing and argument. Not one damn thing! I have busted my ass doing everything you should have been doing to make yourself famous!"

Benjamin wheeled around to face her. "I've done plenty!"

"Writing a few songs in a notebook and screwing another band out of a venue you want in some secret theory you have for overnight success didn't get you far did it? This in front of you right now is only in front of you because I took it upon myself to make it happen."

"You! You are determined to make it about you!"

"It is about me you dumbass! I fronted the money! I got you day jobs! I called in favors and got reviews in papers. I soothed all the feathers you ruffled......."

"No one asked you............."

Danny reached down and picked an ashtray up off the table and threw it into the wall. "No one asked? FUCK YOU! .... Everything I did I did because it became damn clear to me that you weren't going to do anything except become someone no one in this town more that seventy-two hours would work with if their lives depended on it."

"So you say. Yet, when I ask, you can't... or won't................."

"I cannot and I will not blindly sell you out just because you are terrified of success!"

"The truth is that I just can't keep putting my faith in the drunken daughter of some old, drug-addicted, country star.........."

"YOU SON OF A BITCH!"

"Yeah, better a son of a bitch than a daughter of a wash out.........."

With fire in her eyes she turned to face him. In a voice barely more than a whisper she said, "Pack your shit and get the fuck out of my house."

"Gladly."

As Benjamin began to walk from the room, she said, "Oh and Benjamin," he paused but did not turn to face her. "I sincerely hope you make it all the way to the top. Just so you can see how easy it is to fall."

******

Later that week, Conner walked through the doors of the Bomb Shelter. Seeing Gina Marie sitting behind the front desk he said, "Now there is the woman I wanted to see."

Gina Marie looked up and broke into a broad smile. "Really? Why is that?"

"Well there's some celebrating in order and I can't think of a more beautiful woman in the world that I would rather celebrate with."

"Someone seems a bit full of himself today. I think you just might be hanging around Benjamin a bit too much."

"Could be. But if I were you I would be more worried about how much time I spend with Harris."

Gina Marie laughed, "Point taken. So what is it you want to celebrate?

"Well, we just signed with Spat Records. So I wanted to take you out to a really nice dinner."

"You do know Stacy's reputation?"

"Yes. Harris and I discussed it."

"And?" Gina Marie asked taking off her reading glasses.

"And, just between you and me?"

"Of course."

"Stacy knew the conditions that got me and Harris. They are a bit different from Benjamin's agreement."

"Explain."

Conner walked over and sat in a chair across from her. "We tried to talk to Benjamin…….."

"Who hasn't tried to talk to him might be a shorter list."

"So true. Anyway, you have to believe me when I tell you that at no time did Harris and I set out to get the better of Benjamin."

"Oh I believe you. The only one who gets the best of Benjamin is Benjamin."

"Well, when he refused to hear us, we talked with Harris' dad. He told us that when someone refuses to be rescued you have to rescue yourself. So, he helped us to reasonably protect ourselves and still be in a place where we could help Benjamin."

"He'll need someone. I know Danny will be glad to know someone's trying to watch his back."

"That's another reason Harris and I wanted to hang with him. We just felt like we owed her."

"May I tell her that much?"

"Please do."

"You and Harris do realize that even with a better financial arrangement, being associated with Stacy could still be a hit against your careers?"

"We know going in that is a possibility. But the truth is Harris and I love the music. We just want to enjoy the ride, learn and get better at our craft. Harris, well, he's still a kid, he's got time. Me? Well I am a bit older. But I never want music to be lost in the fame.

Besides country music is "forgiving" and one day that is what I plan to play."

"I didn't know that."

"I look at my run with *The Velvet Clutches* and Stacy as sowing my musical wild oats. Now, if you'll have dinner with me I'll let you in on a few more of my secret plans."

"I would love to. But I have to be with Danny. She's taking the break up with Benjamin really hard."

"You know if it hadn't been for you, Harris and I would've never known they separated."

"Doesn't surprise me at all. The longer you know Benjamin, you will find that he says very little that doesn't benefit him. Now, how about a rain check on that dinner?"

"Let's still do it tonight, but with Danny."

"Honey, I know you mean well but rethink that awkward suggestion. Besides, I think the conversation tonight will be strictly girl talk."

"Okay. Tomorrow?" he asked rising to his feet.

"Most definitely," she also got to her feet. "So how'd you get here?"

"Walked some…rode my thumb some…."

Gina Marie grinned. "Let me finish up a few things here, lock up, and I'll give you a ride home, and maybe you'll let me buy you some coffee and pie to celebrate."

"I think my pride could handle that."

******

Nick had sent Gina Marie upstairs. It seemed that Danny hadn't left her bedroom for almost two days now. Gina took a deep breath and opened the door to Danny's room. She stood in the doorway and took in the scene in front of her. It looked as if Danny's closet had exploded. Around the room, half-packed bags sat. Danny sat at her small writing desk. Taking a deep breath of fragile courage, Gina Marie started to speak. Before she could find her voice, Danny saw her and spoke as she rose to her feet. "So glad you're here." She ran over and hugged Gina Marie. As she pulled away, she pushed papers into Gina Marie's hand.

"What are these?"

"My power of attorney and my check books."

"So, it is what it looks like? You're running away."

Danny looked deeply into Gina Marie's eyes. Turning away she walked over to her bed, "What else am I supposed to do?"

Gina heard the tears in Danny's voice. Absently, she shoved the papers into her open purse and dropped the purse onto the floor. "You could stay. Take things head on."

"And how many times have I done that? What does staying end up getting' me?" Danny slammed clothes into her suitcase with each question. Slamming the top down she said, "I'll tell you what it gets me!" she turned to look at Gina, "The same fucking shit over and over again!" She turned back to her suitcase and zipped it shut as she mumbled through tears, "I just know that I can't let it happen to me like it happened to Dad."

Gina Marie stood rooted to her spot. She fought instincts that told her to run to her friend and take her in her arms. Down deep inside, she knew that Danny needed to speak, like lancing a boil, Danny needed to get the poisonous feelings out or else infection would set into her soul and tear at her mind. Quietly, but firmly Gina spoke, "You are not him."

Danny wheeled around and looked at Gina Marie as if she had slapped her for no reason, "Yes, I am! I'm just like him!" She turned around and walked to her dresser, "I'm probably worse." She yanked open a drawer and gazed ahead of her as if she saw something on the wall that no one else could, "Have you ever taken the time to think back and inventory my life? Do you know how many women I called 'Mom'? Six! Six women came after my mother died, that's not including the weekly rotation of girlfriends in and out of my life. And why? Why did I have to suffer through all of them?

Because even though he had me…….. He was still lonely. I wasn't good enough."

She broke her trance- like state and looked over at Gina Marie. "Do you have any idea what it felt – hell, feels like--to know that your dad preferred fake whores who were only interested in their bottom lines and their careers over you?"

"You know I don't."

"You want to know what the complete unfair, insanity of it all is?"

Gina Marie wiped a loose tear from her eyes, "Tell me."

"He was the lucky one! At least he'd known love, he'd known family. And I hate the son of a bitch. I hated him then and I hate him even more now. He knew what it was like to have all my dreams. So, he stole mine when he lost his."

"Danny……………"

"He stole my chances by killing his fucking self. But not right away. Oh no. He couldn't be so merciful as to end it all in one fell swoop. Not my legendary Father." Danny turned her attention to the open drawer and started to pull out items of lingerie.

"Nope, dear old Dad had to kill himself slowly and methodically. One day, one whore, one drink, one drug at a time. Every one of those bitches left one hole after another in his heart, and he stupidly filled those holes with drink and drugs and another bitch!" Danny threw the clothing in her hand at the bed. "And he numbed himself so well that he forgot about me!" She slammed her dresser drawer closed and opened the next one down. "He completely forgot how much I loved him and needed him. I swore Gina," she turned and looked at her friend, "I swore I wouldn't be like him!" Tears streamed from her eyes, "I swore it Gina. I fucking lied to me."

Danny fell back against the wall, "Now, fucking look at me." Slowly, she began sliding down the wall. "Day after fucking day I let myself get sucked into the same shit. I let boy after boy use me for their own selfish gains, and what do I do? I drink away the same pain. I drink away this fucking pain just like he did!" When Danny hit the floor, she wrapped her arms around her knees and buried her face there.

Gina Marie broke her own trance and covered the space between her and her friend in just a few strides. She fell into her knees beside Danny. Wrapping an arm around Danny's shoulder she tried to speak. Again, before she could find words Danny muttered, without raising her head, "Why? Why am I not good enough?"

"You are. Oh, Sweetie, you are a treasure."

Danny raised her head and looked over at Gina Marie. "Then why do I have to buy love with favors and promises of fame like he did? Gina?"

"Yes, Baby."

"Can you tell me why I am not good enough to be loved? What makes me so undeserving?"

"You are good enough. You just set your sights too low that's all. There are more than a couple of us who love you, and I know a few more who respect you and like you for you and....................."

Danny absently opened the bottom drawer a few inches and slid her hand inside as Gina talked. She pulled out a pint of Jack Daniels. "Look at this.... I don't even have a reason to hide it. No one cares how much or when I drink. Yet, just like him I have bottles like these hidden all over this... his...god forsaken house! FUCK!"

Danny slammed the bottle against the dresser. It shattered and the liquor sprayed on both her and Gina Marie. Danny stared at the blood on her hand.

Gina Marie reached up and pulled open a drawer and grabbed a garment from it. She wrapped it around Danny's hand, as Danny cried, "What's wrong with me Gina? What's wrong?"

Gina Marie took Danny into her arms. Rocking her, and through her own tears, Gina whispered "Nothing sweetie. Nothing's wrong. It'll be okay. It's going to be okay."

CHAPTER
EIGHT

8

A year had passed. It was a long year, of playing posh night clubs and dive bars, scattered among the fair grounds and amusement parks. With the always sold out shows, fans screamed for more whenever *The Velvet Clutches* exited the stage and walked out of the clubs. Women were everywhere. CD and merchandise sales were good, reviews were great, that next step--that next album was always an elusive promise made by Stacy.

Conner now knew for sure that Stacy only took them on to get revenge on Danny. He wondered what had passed between them that fueled Stacy forward. He was also glad that Harris' father had gotten them a good deal. He watched as the realization of what he had thrown aside was doing to Benjamin, who was in a downward spiral.

Cold revenge that had led to Benjamin's descent, was what had Conner standing outside a shitty roach motel just outside Atlanta, Georgia on a hot sticky morning pounding on a nasty door. At least they had separate rooms. Thank God for that much. "Benjamin! Come on, Man! Get the fuck up! We need to head out!"

Conner continued to stand waiting. Trying to breath in the water-filled air, he thought of Gina Marie and wondered what she had planned for today. His sweat fueled the flames of anger. He beat the door again. "Come the fuck on man!"

Just as he was about to hit the door again, it swung open and Benjamin stood before him in his black boxer briefs. "What the hell?"

Conner pushed past Benjamin and stormed into the room. "We have to head out to fucking Alabama. We should've been on the road at least a half hour ago."

"You know when Harris wakes me up, he's a lot nicer about it than you are."

"Nice isn't what you need."

Benjamin leaned into the wall. A roach crawled above his head. "He even brings booze."

Conner started grabbing pieces of clothing that were strewn around the room and shoved them into a backpack. "What the fuck did you do in here last night?"

"I don't know; she left about two hours ago."

Conner came across a stack of napkins and scraps of paper with words scribbled on them laying on the nightstand. "Are these important?"

Benjamin pulled himself from the wall and ran across the room. "Yes! Don't fucking touch those! They are my songs." He grabbed them from Conner's hands and plopped himself cross legged on the bed.

To Conner, Benjamin looked like a small boy who was about to lose everything he had left. Conner's tone changed, "We'll look at those in the van. We need to get going." He tossed a t-shirt and a pair of jeans to Benjamin. "Here, get dressed. Be down stairs in ten minutes."

Conner took the backpack with him as he left the room.

******

Harris drove the van forward down the road. Conner sat in the passenger's seat while Benjamin was sprawled across the lone bench seat just behind them.

"I still don't understand why you guys couldn't let me sleep longer where it was more comfortable."

Harris looked into the review mirror, "Quit your whining."

"Fuck you man!"

"No sir. Fuck you."

Conner gritted his teeth, "Come on boys. Knock it off."

Benjamin gave the back of Conner's head a surly look. "Since when did you become the Daddy?"

Harris spoke to Conner, "Just fucking ignore his pansy ass. I think I'll call the guys from Sadaharu and see where we're eating."

Benjamin piped up from the backseat, "Fuck where they're eating. I want McDonalds."

Conner glanced back at Benjamin, "Dude, we've had McDonalds for the last three days."

"So?"

Harris pulled out his cell phone and began to dial hushing the exchange. As the phone rang from behind Benjamin yelled, "Tell them we are going to McDonalds."

To the phone Harris said, "Hey. Where do you guys want to meet up for some lunch? .... Cool, we can do Taco Bell............"

From behind him Benjamin screamed, "I said I want McDonalds!"

Conner turned to Benjamin and growled, "Shut up and act your age."

"Sure, Dude I'll tell them….. Not a problem…….. We're about two exits away now…… Cool, see you in a few minutes." Harris flipped the phone closed and looked at Benjamin in the review mirror, "They said there was McDonalds next door so you can grab what you want there and then come over and join us at Taco Bell."

"I don't want to be the only one eating McDonalds."

Conner groan, "Oh, for God's sake."

Harris couldn't believe his ears, "Dude, are you serious?"

"Fine, do whatever you guys want; I just won't fucking eat."

"That's fine with me. I hope you never eat again."

Conner looked at Harris then back at Benjamin. Taking a very deep breath he snapped, "I'll fucking eat with you okay?"

Benjamin muttered, "Fine."

Harris spat out the word, "Fine."

Conner looked from one to the other and said, "Screw you both."

Harris stared at Conner, "Seriously, it just might come to that if I don't get laid tonight."

Conner groaned, "God oh God," as he hit his head against the window.

******

Harris sat in Taco Bell with Angelo, Jeff, Bill and Mike of *Sadahar*. A laugh erupted just as Conner and Benjamin walked in carrying bags of food from McDonalds.

Conner was in front of Benjamin as they approached the table, "Sup guys? Mind if we join you?"

Angelo looked was the first to look over, "Not at all."

Harris looked over to Angelo with a hurt expression, "Aren't you going to ask my opinion?"

"Fuck no."

"You are an asshole aren't you?"

"I just don't give a damn."

Jeff and Bill had made room and Conner and Benjamin slid in. There were a few minutes of random conversation and private jokes as everyone got there orders together, and began to eat. A napkin was thrown just as a tall, lean man, known to the group of *Sadaharu,* as Jeff S., walked up to their table. "Hey guys, what's up?"

Always the fastest with his mouth, Harris spoke up, "No, we will not watch our language, nor will we be quiet, and I refuse to fucking leave this fine establishment."

Mike threw a packet of sauce at Harris. "Shut up."

Angelo jumped in, "Yeah dude. This isn't some overzealous restaurant manager; this is our label support of the night." He stood up and put an arm around Jeff S. "This everybody is our no suit 'suit' Jeff S. He came all the way down from Lancaster to show us that they still love and care about us." Everyone at the table broke into a laugh. "Okay! Enough already. In all seriousness, he's a chill dude."

Mike still smiling, "Come. Sit. enjoy."

Jeff S. sat next to Harris and Angelo took his seat next to Mike.

Angelo kept the conversation flowing, "So Jeff, I would like to introduce you to our tour mates, *The Velvet Clutches*. Next to you, we have the fastest mouth in the south and the ruling asshole, Harris Tweed, and opposite the other Jeff and Bill, I give you Conner Lee Denton and Benjamin Fiction."

"Nice to meet all of you," Jeff said with a slight nod and wave.

Benjamin looked up from his fries, "Good to meet you."

Sadaharu Jeff looked over at Jeff S., "So Jeff, are you actually going to watch the show tonight or just talk to the fat chicks?"

In response, Angelo quipped, "He's seen us suck enough; I think he's entitled to talk up a 600-pounder if he wants to."

Everyone at the table erupted into laughter. Still snickering Angelo said, "if you're going to watch a show tonight, I would suggest you check out these musical retards."

"Why should I forgo the *B.B.W.'s* in order to listen to these guys?"

Bill spoke up, "Because if you don't, we're going to point you out while on stage and announce that you have herpes."

Sadaharu Jeff piped in, "Yeah, then even the fat chicks won't fuck you."

"You wouldn't?"

Mike looked at Jeff S. with a serious stare, "Remember Boston?"

With mock horror Jeff S. said, "Okay. I'll fucking watch their show."

Angelo looked over to Harris, "See what I fucking do for you guys?"

"Doesn't mean you're not a fucking prick."

Conner looked over at Harris, "It doesn't mean you're not one either."

"Oh fuck you."

Benjamin threw the last bite of his Big Mac down into its box. "I can't eat anymore. The smell of tacos and horse shit are ruining my meal."

Conner looked over at him, "You are just being a big baby today."

Angelo looked around the tables, "Can't we all just get along?"

Harris looked up from his Mexican Pizza, "No. Why should today be different from any other day?"

******

Jeff S. walked up to Benjamin as he came off the stage after *The Velvet Clutches* set. Loud stage music played and sweat poured from Benjamin as Jeff S. handed him a card. "Call me. We'll talk terms."

Benjamin looks at him confused, "What?"

"I'm signing *The Velvet Clutches* to CI Records."

"Really?"

"I don't fuck around with music, just big women. So fucking call me tomorrow."

As Jeff S. walked away, Benjamin looked on in confusion. Conner and Harris walked down the steps of the stage with their equipment.

Conner looked from Jeff's retreating frame to Benjamin, "What did he want?"

"I think he just signed us."

Harris looked at Benjamin and took the card from his hand, "No shit?"

"No shit." Benjamin said in a voice barely more than a whisper.

Sadaharu started to play as the men of *The Velvet Clutches* stood huddled in frozen amazement.

CHAPTER
NINE

Conner walked into the producer's booth of a recording studio to find Benjamin and Harris exchanging icy glares. "What's going on?"

Benjamin looked over at Conner, "He's trying to control the band."

Harris looked up, "Bullshit."

Benjamin looked back to Harris, "Then what would you call what you are doing?"

"Making fucking music magic."

"By destroying the context of my words? You think that's magic?"

"I know it is."

Conner shook his head, "Come on guys, we're nine tracks in. What is there? Two more at most?"

Benjamin looked up, "yeah."

"So let's just get it all done then."

Harris leaned back in his chair, "I'm all for that. I just don't wanna do *Little Razorblade* the way that he wants to. If we play it that damn slow, it's gonna suck."

Conner determined to be Solomon with his fairness shook his head for a few beats before he finally spoke, "Even *Nazareth* did a slow Love Hurts. So, since we paced most of the album your way, Harris, why don't we do this one cut his way and just make it work in the overall."

Resigned Harris said, "Fine. He can be in charge of this one track. But by doing shit like this, we'll become a joke."

Benjamin fired back, "Joke my ass! This shit sells. Have you listened to the radio at all?"

"Fuck no! The radio is the reason music sucks right now."

"Well, people on the radio don't have to sell blood to pay for gas."

"That was one fucking time. Let it go."

Conner who had enough finally lost complete control of his cool, "Guys please! Enough already! *Love Hurts* worked wonders for Nazareth, and *Little Razorblade* like it is, will work wonders for us. Radio or no radio." Clapping his hands together he said, "Now let's get this shit done."

Harris got up from his chair and stormed into the sound booth and sat down at his drum kit.

Conner turned and looked at Benjamin, "You good?"

Benjamin slammed himself into the chair at the sound board. "Let's just get it done." He clicked a button turning on the speaker in the booth. "So, can you try it my way now?"

"One fuck-tarded Ringo coming up."

"You're live. Start when you're ready."

Harris starts playing to the music in his headphones.

Conner looked at Benjamin, "Well the pace is certainly different."

Benjamin looked into the booth and watched Harris play the beat with zero emotion. When Harris noticed him staring, he played the track one-handed while flipping Benjamin a constant bird with the free hand.

Conner conceded, "Well, that takes talent."

"Spare me."

Harris finished the song, dropped his sticks, walked out of the booth through the control room and out the door.

******

Conner and Harris loaded the equipment trailer in the chilly dawn of a December morning. Harris was the first one to speak as he opened the door to the trailer and put in the first of the equipment. "I swear I wouldn't be in a band if it wasn't for all the anonymous sex."

"Oh, really. Why is that?"

"Too much like fucking work. We load and we unload this shit four times a day. Off the trailer into the club, onto the stage, off the stage, back out and onto the trailer. It's just too much like manual labor work. Too fucking much like a real fucking job with shitty hours and crappy pay."

"At least you get to be drunk for most of it," Offered Conner.

"So true. But only when we are laid over or I can talk you into driving. I wonder where Benjamin is. You almost never see him do manual labor."

"Benjamin is the star." They both laughed. "Seriously, he's inside talking with Jeremy."

"Ever wonder what it is they talk about?"

"Not really."

"Me either. But it's nice to know that I'm not the only one who never wonders."

Conner handed up a guitar, "Truthfully it would be nice to be more involved, but too many cooks......... also we are in this together. I mean I've spent more time with you guys in these past two years than with my family. So I look at you two like my brothers. And brothers look out for each other."

Conner passed up the last piece of gear into the trailer and Harris closed the door. "Awww, aren't you so sweet. But you can't possibly be my brother."

"Really, why is that?"

"You don't get laid anywhere near enough."

"Well I have my reasons."

"I know. So what's the deal with that?"

"I don't really know more than that I just really like her."

"Well you certainly do enough of that texting thing with her."

"Yeah I know. I don't understand women's fascination with that."

"It's simple. Women like to drag things out. A fight that should last ten seconds lasts for weeks so they can make 'points'. Sex that should last fifteen minutes has to last hours because 'foreplay; is so important for intimacy. And now they have 'texting'. Now they have found a fucking way to make a five-minute phone conversation last all day. I'm telling you it's all a scheme to make men kill themselves or be forced to surrender into their total control."

Conner laughed, "Where do you come up with this stuff?"

"I think about it during foreplay."

******

As Conner and Harris were loading the trailer, Benjamin was sitting inside at a table across from Jeff S. and Jeremy,an aging rocker and part owner of CI Entertainment and CI Records.

Benjamin looked through the itinerary for *The Velvet Clutches*, "Wow. You've even hooked us up with lodging. The other place left that up to us with a budget based on percentages of the merchandise sales we hawked."

Jeremy and Jeff laughed. Jeremy put his copies of the paper in an old battered file folder, "Well we do our best to take care of our artists especially when they have handed us a near perfect album like you just did. I think you have a natural talent for this."

Benjamin smiled, "I wish I could say that there is something in the water in Nashville, but truthfully it's all about hard work."

"Ten perfect tracks out of eleven is one hell of an average for a group that did its own production work," said Jeff.

"If you don't mind my asking, which track was it that was not quite so perfect?"

Jeremy looked down at another sheet of paper and looked up, "It was track nine, *Little Razorblade*. It's not quite an expected work for this caliber of album."

"I have to agree with Jeremy," Jeff noted. "It sort of threw us a curveball especially when taken with the total album."

"It's not that ball grabbing and it stopped cold the pending orgasm I was about to have listening. I think you could have benefited from carrying something over from the EP instead."

Benjamin paused, and tried to disguise both hurt and the fact that he was taking a deep breath to swallow some anger. Something inside him echoed some all but forgotten words that Danny had said when they had last spoken. "I understand, and to be honest with you I had thought about it, but our old label owns the publishing rights to those and I thought it would have put us over budget to get them back."

Jeff S. looked at Benjamin. He tried to make it clear in the look that he knew it was more than what was being said, then he spoke, "It's part of doing business. From now on you let us worry about things like that. We understand completely and like we said, it's a great overall album. So no worries."

Benjamin stood up from his chair, "Well Gentlemen, I do believe the road calls. Plus I really should be helping with the loading."

Jeff S. and Jeremy both stood and extended their arms across the table they each shook Benjamin's hand.

"Well you boys be safe out there, and we hope to get you back up here this time next year to work on another album." Jeff offered.

Benjamin nodded and left the room.

Jeremy looked to Jeff, "I think that song means something to him."

"So do I."

"All the great rockers had at least one slow one that was a monster hit."

"Yeah, I was thinking the same thing. I think we'll leave it stand but make it the last track on the album."

******

Benjamin walked outside to find the gear already loaded and Conner and Harris leaning against the van smoking cigarettes.

Benjamin called out, "What is it with you? Do you always plan to miss the back-breaking labor that goes into making this band a legacy?"

"Nope, I was just born lucky I guess. Although today I wish I hadn't been."

"Why is that?"

"There's been a bit too much business today."

"Well, sir, that is what you get for stepping up. Come one everyone load in; I'm freezing and I'm driving."

Conner turned and hopped over the trailer hitch and walked to the front of the van. Harris slid open the back door of the van and motioned for Benjamin to jump in, "Are you okay?"

"Yeah."

"Then what's up?"

"Nothing, just a little brain overload."

"Happens to the best of us. That's why they invented this little thing called pussy. It is nature's cure all." Harris slammed the door closed and jumped into the passenger's seat.

******

As they were heading down the interstate toward home, Conner spoke, "So let me get this straight, we have two weeks at home for Christmas, and then we celebrate New Year's with a new album and ten more weeks on the road in the southwest?"

"Yep," Benjamin said from the back.

"Holy fuck me," Harris uttered.

"Agreed," Benjamin responded.

Conner chuckled and looked over at Harris then through the review mirror at Benjamin. "We could always just quit." Harris gave him a weird look as Benjamin leaned forward. "What? It's you guys that are moaning and belly aching."

Benjamin locked eyes with Conner in the review mirror. "Fuck you, Conner."

"I second that." Harris jumped in.

"Then no more complaining from either of you."

Conner leaned forward and wiped some fog from the windshield. "Remember, we are living the dream in its early hours right now."

"Minus the money," Benjamin piped up.

"Minus the fame and the sex."

Harris sat straight up and looked around, "Minus the money, but fucking speak for yourselves when it comes to the fame and the sex. I am living the dream."

CHAPTER TEN

10

The white van pulled up dirty and just as tired as its occupants in the driveway of a dingy, white, two-story house with the detached garage. Benjamin's ancient Lexus was sitting off to the side. Harris, Conner and Benjamin all pulled themselves from the van the second it came to a stop.

"Home sweet home," Harris said as his feet hit the driveway.

Conner looked up at the tired edifice and said, "Damn, I never knew a shit hole like this could look so good."

"Hey, if this place is going to start looking good to you how about paying some rent?"

Conner laughed, "That's funny Harris. You should put together an act and take it on the road."

"What did I say that was so funny? I only spoke the truth."

Conner reached out and patted Harris on the shoulder, "Don't worry, suddenly this place has lost all its charm."

"Asshole."

"I'll get my things later. Right now that mattress on the floor is calling my name." Conner walked away and headed toward the house.

Benjamin turned to look at Harris, "Mind jumping me off if my car doesn't start?"

"Yeah, Man… no problem."

"I've gotta go see if my mom will have me back until I find a more suitable living arrangement."

"I thought you were shacking up with that blond."

"I was. Then I decided to disappear for two thirds of the year, and she found another dick."

"Well, that wasn't too smart on someone's part."

"I just don't know whose part."

"Why don't you forget the car and your mom? I've got a spare room or two."

Benjamin chuckled. "I don't know man. I love my mom's cooking, but still my shit is already here in my car."

"So it comes down to if you feel like driving some more."

"Not really. I'm still going to see my mom no matter what. I need my laundry done."

"Well it's not perfect here, but it is fun," Harris said. "We have a few musicians here and a drug dealer. Girls come by all the time. There's always beer. The only problem is that I have Jay in the garage."

"Jay? Really? I thought he went to Seattle."

"He did. But he came back and needed a place so he remembered the Hollywood House and gave me a call. Remember this about me if you remember nothing else. I never turn away a struggling musician, alcohol in all its intoxicating forms or a hot piece of pussy."

Benjamin laughed again, "I guess that's pretty cool of you."

"It is one of my more enduring charms. So? What's it gonna be? The lonely highway or a night at The Hollywood House?"

"Why the hell not!"

"Cool, Brother. Welcome to me casa."

"You actually call this place the Hollywood House?"

"It wasn't my idea. But this is where all the cool and trendy shit goes down. Or at least I'm told that."

"You really got a live-in dealer?"

"Yes I do. Pays his rent in stash."

"I guess this place couldn't be more audacious."

"This place is the height of decadence. And that's Hollywood."

"Sounds fun."

"Among other things. Let's go see who all is here.

******

Benjamin entered the foyer of Danny's home through the front door. He stood there for a minute and looked around. His memories rambled until Nick walked in from the living room.

"Hey, Benjamin. I thought I heard someone."

"The door was unlocked."

"Happens sometimes. Listen if you are looking for something you might have forgotten I am pretty sure that Danny has burned it or donated it by now."

"No actually I was hoping to give her something."

"Oh. Well I am pretty sure she's up in her room. You remember where that is right?"

A faint smile played on Benjamin's lips, "Yeah, I do. So, it's alright if I go on up?"

"Don't see why not."

Benjamin started toward the stairs. Nick's voice stopped him. "Hey, congrats on the new album deal."

"Thanks."

"I bet it feels nice to be out from under Stacy's thumb."

"Yeah. We're free, but our music isn't. But we'll get there."

"Hope you do."

Nick walked back toward the living room as Benjamin went up the steps two at a time. He walked slowly down the hall and stopped in front of Danny's room. Taking a deep breath he knocked softly on her door. When he got no answer he quietly opened the door. Cautiously he entered her room to find her in her bed. He walked over and sat on the edge of her bed and watched her sleep for a second before noticing her nightstand arrayed with a bottle of Rock Hill bourbon, an overflowing ashtray and a mirror with a dusting of coke on it.

"Danny," he whispered.

Reaching out slowly, he placed his hand on her forehead and brushed back her bangs with his thumb. Slowly he allowed his hand to run down her cheek. He stood up and pulled a press of the new CD out of his pocket and placed it against her bottle of bourbon. He looked at her for another minute before bending down and once more softly brushing back her hair. Slowly and tentatively, he placed a kiss on her cheek.

"I really suck don't I? I lied to you, used you. But yet you never stopped loving me and I'll admit to it, but every bit of talent that I have came from simply trying to impress you. I love you, and the sad thing is that you'll never know how much. It wasn't your fault we ended even if it feels that way. It was all me. I just wish that I was man enough to tell you this to your face."

He continued to gaze at her. Tears filled his eyes, blurring his vision. "If for one moment, I believed I could fix myself we would have a chance to make it. I love you, Baby Doll. And I always will."

Benjamin stood up straight and walked for the door turning only briefly to take one last look before he closed her door.

******

Conner sat shirtless on the edge of Gina Marie's bed listening to the shower run. He looked over in the corner and noticed a guitar on a stand. He got up and walked the short distance to pick it up. He examined it closely and walked absently back toward the bed. He sat there and played a few chords listening to the sweet sounds the Martin made. After a moment he started to put together the chords into beautiful notes. The notes turned to a tune and the tune was filled with words, words that were filled with a tenor voice that would make any Irishman cry.

"My pa took off by the time I learned to ride a bike.

Left nothing to me but my last name.
So with nowhere else to go
Mamma's '88 Oldes
Pointed straight to granddaddy's driveway.

He said welcome home Kentucky boy,
So good to see your face again.
Kick off your shoes and stay awhile.
And look how much you've grown.
My, it's been a long time.
So welcome home Kentucky boy………"

"What song is that?"

Conner stopped playing and looked up at her with guilt in his eyes. "You startled me."

"I didn't mean to interrupt. That was beautiful."

"Sorry to pick this beauty up. I hope I am not overstepping. It's just this is a beautiful piece of workmanship and it's……….."

"Don't worry about it. That song Conner, that song was wonderful."

"Oh, it's nothing; it's just something I've been working on."

"You wrote it?"

"Yeah, well writing it actually."

Gina Marie walked across the room and knelt behind Conner on the bed and put her arms around his neck and kissed his cheek. "It feels like I have known that song forever."

"And it feels like I've been singing it forever."

"You really should work more on your stuff."

"You think so?"

"Yes. And you have a great voice to go with the stuff you do like, what are you doing playing bass in a rock band?"

"I just followed where old Nashville led me."

"Maybe you should stop following."

"Maybe I will. If we ever take a break."

"Well I hope you take a break soon. I'd love to hear more of your music."

"And I'd love to play more for you."

"Tomorrow though. Right now I want you to come back to bed with me."

Conner sat the guitar against the nightstand and rolled into the bed next to Gina Marie and pulled her to him.

CHAPTER
ELEVEN

11

It was the day after Christmas, and the main bar area at the Gold Rush was packed. In two days *The Velvet Clutches* would be heading out of Nashville and getting back on the road again to play higher-class establishments all across the desert southwest. The atmosphere was light and the band mates sat with their dates, Gina Marie and Benjamin with his new blonde of the moment. Nick and Sarah were also there as were friends Matt B., Davis, and Brandon Jazz.

Suddenly, Harris being Harris jumped up onto the table and began shouting, "Ladies, gentlemen and perverts alike! May I have your attention?" The bar noise died down and all eyes were cast on Harris. "I am Harris Tweed, and whether you know it or not it's a pleasure to meet me. I would like to thank you all for being here to celebrate my band, *The Velvet Clutches* heading back out onto the road. I know most of you didn't come here intending to celebrate that..... actually it was just this table here that came here with that purpose in mind. But now you know that you are a part of the celebration. So, feel free to ply us with free congratulatory alcohol. Thank you one and all and by the way we are available to sign autographs, and take pictures."

Harris hoped off the table and sat down. Gina Marie looked at him and asked, "What was that about?"

"That was about being broke and needing more alcohol. You'll see. None of us will have to pay for anything the rest of the night, and of course, you'll have to drink what they send."

Nick looked at Harris, "I don't see it working that way."

Harris smiled, "Oh ye of little faith."

Benjamin's new blonde friend piped in, "Are you all something special?"

Harris smiled back at her, "No more special than you are sweetheart."

"Awww, thanks."

Benjamin pointed behind Harris to a waitress carrying a tray of shots. "I don't know what it is, but that boy has something about him," he said to everyone at the table.

Harris turned to meet the tray and took two shots immediately downing one and replacing the empty onto the tray. When the table had been served, he held the other shot glass up and looked over at Conner. "Conner, you're the more wordly elegant one so what are we toasting to?"

Conner raised his glass as did the rest of the table. "It may be a few days off, but this one is to the New Year. May it bring whatever the hell we want it to."

Those at the table whooped their agreement and slammed back the shots. Gina Marie reached down and picked up her phone and looked at the screen. She turned to Conner, "I've gotta return this call, Babe. Can you let me slide out?"

"No problem, is everything okay?"

Gina Marie whispered, "It's Danny," in his ear, and left the table.

Conner got back in his seat and turned his attention back to the others. "So, Brandon, tell me about this new band of yours, what is it called? *The Armed Forces?*"

******

Danny was standing over her bed. She was picking from neatly folded clothing and peacefully packing the items in her suitcase when her phone rang. She reached over and pressed the speaker button as she checked the caller I.D., "Hey Gina, you didn't have to call me back. I left you a message."

"I didn't bother with checking the message. So what's going on?"

"I'm going to L.A. for a few days."

"Why? What's going on?"

"I'm going to see Dan. I need to call in a favor with him."

"Please tell me it ain't............."

"It is."

"Oh, Danny, he's not worth it. Trust me on that one."

"I'm not doing it for the reasons that you are thinking. I'm doing it because I have to finish it. Finish what I started…….."

"Danny……………"

"No listen to me. I can't close this chapter unless I finish what I started and this has been the last part of every plan since I met him. I have to do it."

"Do you need a traveling buddy?"

"No. I'll be fine."

"Okay, Sweetie. But promise me if it does fix most of it you're going to do what we talked about."

"I promise. If it doesn't end up helping, I'll check myself in."

"Whether it helps or not you're checking yourself in. Promise."

"I promise."

"Okay. Then fly safe."

"I will. I love you."

"I love you too."

Danny reached over and turned off the speaker phone. "Lord help me. I pray this is the right thing to do."

******

Benjamin tossed and turned, on a ratty old couch in the den of The Hollywood House, trying to hold on to the fragile pieces of sleep, when he got pulled back to earth by the buzzing of his cell phone vibrating on the coffee table. He moaned and rolled over just as the buzzing stopped. A few seconds passed then the buzzing starts again. Benjamin sat straight up and grabbed the phone.

"What!"

At the other end of the phone Dan Catullo sat at his desk in a low rent office in Los Angeles. "Is this Benjamin Fiction?"

"Yeah. Who wants to know?"

"This is Dan Catullo. Sorry to wake you. I just wanted to tell you that I heard your album.... Well, actually both of them. And I'd like to talk to you about representation for *The Velvet Clutches*."

"Well I kind of handle that. Besides we're already signed."

"I see that. With CI Entertainment?"

"Yeah."

"You can do better than them. Well, slight correction. I can get you better."

"Really?"

"I have a slot open for a label showcase out here at The Viper Room. It's yours if I'm your manager."

"Are you for real?"

"Yes, this is for real."

"How?"

"Does it really matter? I mean we're talking a chance to play for major labels."

"Look I'm going to be honest here. I am hung over and worn out. Getting' ready to head out on the road on tour. So let's say this isn't a joke. Explain it a little better for me."

"Jason Hollis gave me your music. I'm a producer and talent agent. I mainly do DVD's. But if I manage you, I can get you a spot on the stage at The Viper Room playing for A and R scouts for the major labels. If you tour at all in the early months, it will be here in California. That's as clear as it gets."

"I know Jason."

"I don't like to waste time. Say yes or no."

"The tour……"

"If you agree with me now, I will call CI and work out the details for your band to be here in Los Angeles in a week to play at The Viper Room for a couple of nights."

"Yeah…… Sure….."

"Good. Plan to be in Los Angeles in a week's time. Someone from CI will be calling you shortly with the details."

"Cool. We'll be there."

Benjamin snapped his phone shut and looked around the dingy room. He ran his hand through his hair. He stood up and slipped slipped his phone in his pocket and headed out of the room calling for Harris and Conner as loud as he could.

******

Danny sat on the couch in the living room of Jason Hollis home. She stared out the floor to ceiling windows at the ocean. Malibu was a beautiful place. And to think it was her wheeling and dealing that bought him this view. Jason, a bleach blonde surf bum with a southern accent was on the phone. She listened to his voice; she had always liked the sound of his voice.

He clicked off on his phone and looked at her, "It's done. They're in."

"Divine."

"Apparently Benjamin's a hung over prick."

"Always."

"You sure can pick 'em."

"I picked you didn't I?"

"Touché'." Jason moved closer to her and put his arm around Danny. He leaned over and barely kissed her lips. Abruptly she stood up.

"You are a married man."

"So?"

"So. We didn't work before and we are not going to work now."

"So that's the way it works is it? I do you a favor and….."

"And what? You just paid an overdue debt. You shouldn't be sitting here and you know it. If it weren't for me you would be either playing in the alleys of Nashville or hanging ten in the surf out there sleeping under the stars."

"Hey whoa…. When did you become a bitch?"

"The day you dumped me. I'm out of here."

Danny left the room and he heard her slam out the front door. In frustration and anger Jason kicked the coffee table over, and fell onto the couch nursing a hurt toe.

CHAPTER
TWELVE

In some small town about a hundred miles outside of Phoenix, the tour van of *The Velvet Clutches* sat dusty and hot. A fresh tank of gas, windows cleaned, water topped off and it was ready to go. Harris and Conner walked out of a gas station's mini mart towards the van; their arms loaded with chips, beer, soda and an enormously large jar of beef jerky.

"Dude, if fake tits look that good in Phoenix I can't wait to see the ones out in Hollywood."

"Harris, that woman was 60 if she was a day."

"I know, I know it's kinda like putting a new door on a house that's falling apart but still, good work is good work and a failure to recognize it is an insult to artistry."

Conner shook his head, "I don't know about you Harris. Sometimes I wonder what those hippies were thinking when they had you."

"It had to be the pot or maybe the LSD that created me. I am without a doubt one in a million."

Conner sat the beer and soda down by the van as he slid open the door. "You are without a doubt one in something that's for sure…….. Hey Benjamin."

"Yo ho-ho sleeping beauty. Time to rise, shine and take a piss."

"Come on Benjamin. Go take a dump and wash up only a few hundred more miles to go."

"Yeah, you want to look your best when you hit the sunset strip."

Benjamin sat up and rubbed the sleep from his eyes. "What are you guys my parents?"

Harris laughed. "Someone has to take care of you."

Benjamin looked at the large jar of jerky cradled in Harris's arms. "What the hell is that?"

"Homemade jerky. It is to die for let me tell you."

"And how much did you waste on it?"

"Hey, I got a great deal."

Conner interrupted, "Believe me, you don't wanna know the details of that deal."

Benjamin pulled himself out of the van and walked towards the side of the station where the restrooms were.

Harris called out after him. "Hey Dude, don't forget to wipe your pussy when you're done."

Benjamin holds his hand up flipping Harris off as he walked on without looking back.

******

In Los Angeles for two days now, Benjamin, Conner and Harris all lounged around a small, hot, one-room apartment above Dan Catullo's recording studio. The friends were more than a little grumpy, hungry and broke. They were doers forced to do nothing.

Harris sat up from his pallet on the floor in front of a fan. "God Damn! I think we are in hell."

Conner who was strumming his acoustic never looked up, "Not………."

"Shut the hell up. Don't you dare say paradise again. This is hell."

Benjamin, who lounged on the recliner, opened his eyes, "It's better than the van Harris."

"The van has air."

Conner snickered, "Like we have money for the gas to run it."

Harris looked from one to the other of his band mates, partners and sometimes friends. "For two guys who want to manage us they sure as hell don't want to keep us alive."

Benjamin popped his recliner from fully reclined to semi, "Think of this as a journey, no, a bump in the road of our journey. This is the unpleasant part of a golden opportunity we are being given. We are going to be playing in The Viper Room, in front of major label A and R's."

Conner looked over at Benjamin as Harris rolled his eyes, "Yeah, about that. I get that our style is audacious, but seriously are we ready for a major label yet?"

Benjamin looked over at Conner, "Probably not."

"So why exactly………."

"So, why what? Why not? I mean those ghetto ass rappers do it all the time. From the projects to mansions. Why not some pasty-ass white boys?"

Harris piped in, "The pasty ass white boy has a point."

Benjamin looked over at Harris, "Shut the hell up."

"Fuck your mother's ass without a rubber…………"

"Hey!" Benjamin exclaimed as he popped his recliner to fully upright.

"Sorry. I forgot... She's a saint and you're The Immaculate Conception."

Conner got to his feet, "Whatever," he looked from one to the other. "Remember guys, going with the flow has worked so far. What was it we agreed on in the beginning? We may not be the best, but we sure as hell are the greatest."

Harris shook his head. "We didn't agree on that. I said that about myself."

"Really?"

Harris nodded, "We are still in hell……" he said as he lay back down.

"Why don't you take a walk if you're that uncomfortable?"

"Cause Conner, I am waiting for the pizza, beer, cigarettes and other assorted munchies that Dave is bringing. Then I am out of here. Priorities man. You have to get your priorities in order."

******

The uncharacteristic heat of the day had given itself to the cool fingers of the night. And on this night Jason Hollis and Danny walked across a parking lot filled with black BMW's and Mercedes. The occasional Jag screamed for look at me status as the two walked in silence.

Jason turned to look at Danny. "Okay, so the plan is that when we get in there, I will intro you to Dan and he'll take you around to all the majors so you two can sell the guys."

As they reached the street, Danny stopped so quickly that she caused Jason who had her arm to trip. He stopped and looked at her, "What's wrong? Are you alright?"

Staring straight ahead into nothingness, Danny said in a low pain filled voice, "He doesn't need me."

Jason wasn't sure he heard her right. Hell, he wasn't sure he had heard her at all. The tone in her voice was of one that had just recognized an intrinsic truth that awed them. But not being a man of compassion much less mysticism his response was a short, "What?"

Slowly still staring Danny shook her head and answered as if she were talking to someone just in front of her, "They don't need me."

He heard a bit of pain in her voice with those words. However, that didn't change who he was much less his demeanor. All he knew was that they were now running a bit behind, and he was a stickler to schedules. He took a deep breath in an effort to steady himself and his words, "What are you talking about? They wouldn't be here without you."

Her trance ending, Danny snapped to herself and looked over at Jason, "No. I'm not going in there." She said pointing across the street at The Viper Room.

"What......................"

"Fuck it. I don't care. Just give me your keys." Jason was stunned and looked at her in puzzlement.

When he made no move at all Danny shouted, "Give me your god damned keys!"

Jason fumbled in his pockets and came up with the keys and offered them to her.

Danny reached out and grabbed them from his hands. "When you get there, you and Dan watch. Nothing else. They'll get noticed. They don't need you or me. You're done. More importantly I'm done. Now get in there and do only what your contracts require. Nothing more."

Jason confused, continued to stare blankly at her.

"Go Jason. Go now! Watch a miracle unfold. And monitor the paperwork. Nothing more."

Jason began to move across the street as Danny quickly hurried back across the parking lot, anger in her eyes, resolve in her heart. She got into the car and put the keys in the ignition and took off.

******

The Velvet Clutches were on the stage behind the curtain at The Viper Room, Dave Paulson stood with them.

Benjamin peeked out the curtain and looked at the others, "God, it's like a Blackberry user convention out there."

Harris smiled, "Suits and their blueberries. By far one of our more tamed crowds."

Dave looked at Harris, "It's black…….."

Conner looked at Dave and shook his head, "Don't bother, Man; he worked for more than three seconds on that one."

Harris continued on talking to Benjamin as if the other two had said not one word. "Don't freak Benjamin. We got this. Granted, I thought that a Hollywood audience would be silicon boobies. But we'll go out there and slay those blueberries."

Benjamin looked at Harris, "This could be our only chance…….."

"Maybe yours. But this time being my only chance does not fall into my plans anywhere at all."

Benjamin looked around at the three of them, "Does anyone got any blow?"

Dave reached into his pocket and handed Benjamin a small baggie. Which he quickly opened and dipped a finer into. He snorted a bump.

Harris reached out, "Share the shit."

Benjamin handed Harris the small bag. Harris shook a small amount on the back of his hand and snorted as he handed the bag back over to Dave who did the same before offering the bag to Conner.

Harris spoke up, "No man, he doesn't do that shit."

Conner looked around at his friends, "Wait... why not? I can't think of a better time to start."

Everyone watched as he took the bag and nervously stuck his finger in and scooped a generous bump.

Just as Conner started to snort Harris said, "Wait……………"

Snorting quickly Conner looked over to Harris, "What?"

Harris looked at everyone, "Well, this night just got interesting."

Conner looked around, "Are we ready to do this?"

Benjamin was the first one to answer, "Fuck, no; no," just as the curtains parted.

******

Conner sat on a curb in back of *The Viper Room*. A dim streetlamp flickered above his head, while a cigarette burned in his hand. Harris came out the back door.

"There you are."

"Here I be."

Sitting down next to Conner, Harris started talking, "You know we killed it in there. We're going to be famous for all of fifteen minutes, just like MC Hammer."

"That's good."

"You're kinda fucked up aren't you?"

"I love Gina Marie."

"Yep. You're fucked alright."

Conner wiped at his blood shot eyes. "Should we go in there?"

"Normally I'd say yes because you're the one we depend on making a good impression. In this case, however, let's keep you out here for a while longer."

"I'm glad I met you."

"Same here Buddy."

"I want to do some more coke."

"Maybe in a day or two. You did enough for your first time."

Conner fell over into Harris' lap. "That's not exactly the head I wanted in my lap tonight." Harris reached over and grabbed the cigarette out of Conner's hand and took the last puff off it before he flicked it into the middle of the abandoned area.

Conner opened an eye and looked up at Harris, "I love you Harris."

Harris looked down, "If you ever say that with your head in my lap again I'll be forced to kill you. But the truth is that I love you too."

CHAPTER
THIRTEEN

13

Harris, Conner and Benjamin stood in the elevator of Geffen. Up above them was awaiting a meeting of a lifetime. This was it, the big time called to them, and they were on their way up to face it head on and get on with a success that in each of their hearts not a one of them expected. But they had ridden the course and taken it all one day at a time. Not even Conner knew that an unsuspecting angel had cleared the way. If they had, it would have changed anything? Later, when Conner was to find out, this was a question that would nag at him for the rest of his life.

Harris was the first to speak, "So these are the guys?"

Benjamin just looked ahead and nodded his head.

It was Conner that answered Harris' question and Benjamin's nod with a simple, "Cool."

"These are the ones that want to talk with us about signing right?" Again Benjamin merely nodded to Harris' question. "But I thought we had already decided to sign and you had told them so."

"I told them we would be interested as a group to hear more."

The elevator stopped and the guys got out to be greeted by a receptionist. "*The Velvet Clutches*, I presume?" They all nodded as one. "Right this way, Gentlemen." She turned and began to walk away and they fell in suit.

Harris whispered, "That's a great ass."

Benjamin elbowed him in the gut. Conner gave him a sharp look. With his hand on his waist, Harris had no choice but to walk on. The receptionist opened a door at the end of the hall and motioned the trio into a conference room. The room was anchored by a huge table in the center of the room and sitting in all but three chairs were label executives. The table itself was piled with fruits, pizza, and muffins. At the head of the table was Sam Jordon. He got to his feet as they walked into the room.

"Welcome," Sam said in a very assured tone as he rounded the table to shake hands with the men. "How are you gentlemen doing on this fine day?"

"Good and you?" Benjamin asked as he shook his hand.

"Great. Great. Glad to have you boys here."

Harris looked at the food-laden table and the open wet bar behind it and smiled, "It looks like you already knew we were signing with you."

"I won't lie, I was hoping that we would be celebrating at this meeting and ironing out details. Like where you boys are going to live while we cut the next album and work up a promotional touring agenda."

Sam turned to face the room, "Ladies and gentlemen, I'd like for you to meet our newest recording artists."

Turning back he looked at the trio, "Come enjoy the refreshments and meet your new best friends. Once everyone is acquainted we have what I hope will be a huge surprise for you gentlemen."

Benjamin headed straight for the table and began introducing himself. Harris looked at Conner and whispered, "I hope the surprise is a strip club."

"Strip club?"

"Yeah, you gotta love my thinking. I have always wanted to snort a line off a stripper's ass........ Again."

Sam looked over at Harris and broke into a wide smile. This one he thought to himself, I will enjoy having around. "Don't be silly. You aren't quite old enough for strip clubs young man. We're going to Disney."

Conner wasn't entirely sure this was a joke. He privately hoped it was and in a sense of playing along he said, "Oh boy Mickey Mouse, tea cups and rock 'n' roll."

Harris looked at Sam, also not sure, then he looked over at Conner, "Don't worry, dude; there are ladies at Disney, some of them real princesses."

******

The studio owned an old hotel that had been converted into studio apartments, and that is where the guys were sent to live side-by-side, until certain details could be worked out. Benjamin had called Conner and Harris to his apartment. Harris stood outside the closed door and knocked. Conner answered the door.

"Quick response time. Nice to see no gayness happening between you two." Harris walked in.

Conner whispered to Harris, "Chill it with the comments. Benjamin's just not in the mood today."

Benjamin looked up at Harris, "Shut up Harris. You know my standards are not that low."

Conner turned around and looked at Benjamin, "Well, thanks a lot."

Harris plopped down on the floor and looked over at Benjamin, as Conner came in and sat on the opposite end of the couch. "So, what's with disturbing me? And believe me you really are keeping me from something special."

"Forgive me for pulling you out of your hepatitis ridden hole."

"Hey! It may be dirty. But the mess keeps me close to my roots."

Conner looked down at Harris, "What's her name?

"Melissa Bamberg."

"Not that it matters, but where did you meet her?" Benjamin asked, pretending to be interested.

"Remember that whatever event we played at The Viper Room a few weeks ago?"

"Oh, is she one of the twins that you took home?"

"Nope. But she was there and then later she found me on MySpace and messaged me asking if I'd like to get together and fuck."

"I hope she doesn't turn psycho and cut off your dick," Conner said.

"Well she's had plenty of chances already and the mini me is safe, sound and quite happy."

"You're insane."

"Hardly. But I am a bit raw…………"

Benjamin interrupted, "Okay! Enough already. The reason I called you guys here was to let you know that the label got Jeff Bebe to produce our next album."

Harris looked up in shock, "The guy from *The Vans?*"

"The same. But there's a catch."

"Oh man! Nothing this sweet is ever this pure," moaned Conner.

"What's the catch?"

"We're going to have to move to New York for a while to do the recording."

Harris moaned. "We have to go from sunny and fake to real and gloomy. Do we have a choice in the matter?"

Benjamin and Conner both looked at him like he had lost his mind. Benjamin spoke, "We are talking about the same dude behind *Bad Religion* and *Weezer*."

Harris broke into a smile. "I was kidding. Damn, so when do we leave?"

CHAPTER
FOURTEEN

14

The trip from Los Angeles to New York was a book of adventures, attitude and latitudes in and of itself. They argued, they sang, they slept, and it was Conner and Harris that did all the driving. When Benjamin wasn't complaining, he was sleeping. They drove mind numbing mile after mind numbing mile. It seemed that flying, which was offered to them as an option, was not something that Benjamin was 'up' to. Conner made careful note after note. He fully intended to write a book about this one day, and from the way the notes were stacking up, the trip from California to New York was going to be a volume in and of itself.

Their arrival in New York was nothing to write home about. Benjamin was in a mood and none of them had been in a city quite like this one. The traffic was a nightmare; the parking was a horror film. Finally, they arrived at the studio, met Jeff Bebe and were pointed to a two bedroom apartment, to lay their heads and a parking garage six blocks from the apartment. Harris was like a kid in a candy store, and to keep all peace and maybe get some for himself, Conner let the other two have the bedrooms, he occupied the couch.

On their first night in New York City, Jeff and his wife took the three to an upscale restaurant. It was small talk all the way around as they placed their orders and sipped their drinks.

Taking a deep breath, Jeff was the first to speak at all about business, "I am going to cut to the chase. The only reason I agreed to produce your album is because I heard your first album and in one word it is "great" for a shitty little indie label. However, I and you, on this, your freshmen big league effort, are going to be epic."

Harris looked up, "But, I already am epic."

Benjamin looked mortified and glared at Harris, "Shut…….."

"No, no. I like that attitude." Jeff said raising a hand at Benjamin's protest. "That's what it takes to be great in this industry. All this humble crap you hear from the big names in this business is shit. Just plain old horse shit. I promise you, all of them have the same attitude when the cameras aren't around. Trust me I should know I am one of those arrogant assholes."

With that, everyone relaxed and the meal was a calming success of business mixed with getting to know you pleasure.

Later, back in their little apartment Conner, Harris and Benjamin sat around the living room passing a mirror with lines of welcome to New York coke. Each took a healthy snort before Harris lay the mirror on the coffee table.

Conner leaned back and let the words, "Epic, huh?" float freely from his mind and out of his mouth.

"That is what the man said," Benjamin said lighting a cigarette.

"I like it. Epic should be a song we write just for the occasion, maybe it should even be the album's title," said Harris as he lay back on the floor.

Conner was more contemplative, and his next thought showed that, "It's a nice idea, a wonderful thought. Epic. But honestly how many epic bands are there?"

Benjamin leaned back and looked up following a smoke ring as it floated toward the ceiling, "*The Rolling Stones.*"

Conner looked over at him, "Really? I mean are they truly epic? Or is it that they just lasted the longest?"

Harris rose up on an elbow, "I think *The Kinks* are epic."

Conner looked over in his general direction, "True. I mean no disrespect to Jagger, but how many other bands has he truly influenced? *The Kinks* though......"

Benjamin spoke as if to no one at all, "*Beach Boys.*"

Harris broke into a huge grin, "I love the *Beach Boys.*"

"Me too," agreed Conner.

Harris was the next to pose a question, "So does that make them epic? The fact that we all love them?"

Benjamin and Conner looked to one another. There was a moment of silence as if everyone wanted to pause and give this question serious thought before answering. Finally it was Conner that broke the silence, "If you go by Jeff, we're 'epic' enough to declare others epic."

Harris sat up and looked at Conner, "Then damn it, I declare MC Hammer epic."

All of them smiled, and Benjamin looked at Harris then over to Conner. "I hereby declare Harris to be an epic fuck-tard."

They all laughed, "And I humbly accept your declaration. You give out so few...... so Benjamin, what did you think about Jeff's wife?"

"Hot as hell."

Harris looked over to Conner, "Conner? What did you think?"

"I have no opinion."

Benjamin looked over at Conner, "My god, Gina has you whipped."

"Shut up Benjamin, I think it's sweet the way Conner feels. Does my heart good. Besides how is it any different from your and Danny's former relationship?"

Benjamin gives Harris the dirtiest of dirty looks. "So, I got her number."

Conner looked over, "Whose number?"

"The wife…Anita."

Now, it was both Conner and Harris who cut sharp dirty looks to Benjamin. Harris was the first to speak, "To be clear, are you talking about Jeff's wife?"

"Have we met any other Anita's?"

"You fucking asshole!" Conner got up from the couch and walked over to the window, "There's nothing dumber that you could've possibly done."

"What? It's not like I asked her for it. She gave it to me."

Harris looked from one friend to the other, "Okay. Seriously, for a minute, let's all be serious. I am the king of…. Well let's just say that I make a lot of bad choices when it comes to the ladies. But shit man. If you use that number. It's going to be a bad choice. Not just for you but for all of us."

"Will you both just chill? I am not going to use the number. I just said that she gave it to me."

Conner continued to stare out the window, he muttered, "Good."

Harris lay back down, "Good is right."

******

It was about three days later when, Jeff Bebe stormed into a studio at the Electric Lady, while Benjamin, Conner and Harris were in the middle of recording. He grabbed his laptop off the sound board and turned to walk out. As he got to the door he stopped, turned back and opened the door of the recording studio mid-song surprising the trio.

"Benjamin! The next time you fuck a guy's wife. Make sure he can't fuck you back." Jeff stormed out again, leaving Conner and Harris standing there staring at Benjamin.

Benjamin looked at his friends, "Fuck."

Conner took off his guitar, he calmly laid it down, and he turned into Benjamin's face, "Fuck is right."

Harris sensed a need to lighten the room, "I can't really fault you for doing what I would have done......."

Conner looked at Harris, then back into Benjamin's eyes, "Fuck!"

Harris lit a cigarette, "Do we still have a job?"

Through the speakers the sound engineer broke in, "Nope."

Harris looked over to Benjamin and Conner, "Well, Benjamin, all I can say is fuck you!"

Benjamin looked over at Harris, "Shut up."

"Shut up?! You just fucking cost us everything and you tell me………………"

"Do you honestly think I don't know what I did?"

"Please! It's always about you! What you want. And we are supposed to shut up and understand. Well today you cost all of us. So fucking fuck you!" Harris flicks his cigarette in Benjamin's face and walks out.

Benjamin turned to Conner who was still just inches from his face, "Are you planning to join him?"

"Just tell me why. Why do you have to destroy everything and everybody good around you? Why?"

Benjamin just stared blankly at Conner. The seconds ticked by. Finally it was Conner that spoke, "I'm sorry for you. " He turned and picked up his bass and walked over to put it in its case. Closing the case he walked past Benjamin to the door, at the door he stopped and said without turning around, "Find your own way home man. I don't think we either one can stand to be that close to you." With that he walked out the door leaving Benjamin standing in the studio alone.

CHAPTER
FIFTEEN

15

Benjamin made it back to Nashville. The trip was via train then via bus because he got bored. The truth, many truths revealed themselves to him on his journey home. He knew it was too late to ever redeem himself as a front man. Or at least that's what he knew right now. He knew he'd have to beg for a bar gig, maybe freelance as a producer. Take all that, Harris had taught him to be content with being a writer. He knew that because of some uncontrollable, compelling desire to destroy himself he had screwed up, not so much with the affair, as miscalculating her husband. He paid no attention to the man in the situation. If he had, he would have noticed that the man loved his wife. Love was something that was rare these days in this business he had become too jaded to see it and notice its existence.

Notice its existence. That thought played with his mind for most of his trip and the week he had hidden himself away at his mother's house. Benjamin was many things, arrogant, short sighted, selfish, self-absorbed and the list went on and on. But the one thing no one realized about him was the one thing that kept him moving, he was a sponge, he remembered everything, every nuance, every conversation. And he was logical. So when he screwed up bad enough, he always ended up sitting up and replaying everything. Not just what went wrong but all the events that had led him there.

And there it was in the cold replay. In the searing light of day. Though no one would ever admit it, he knew in his heart of hearts that with Danny he had, had it all, and that because of Danny, he had been given the chance to have it all. He also knew that she loved him, and that the emptiness he felt inside was because he had loved her, and he had lost her. All the data reviewed, all the new insights learned, propelled him to move forward in a vastly different direction, and propel him forward it did.

He drove to Nashville, and drove on to Danny's house. He walked through her unlocked front door, and walked right on up the curved staircase, down the hall and stopped only when he reached her bedroom door. Her door was ajar, and he looked in at her for a moment. She sat on her bed writing in a spiral notebook or maybe it was a day planner, either way his breath was taken away by her beauty as she sat there.

Danny sensing someone staring at her looked up startled, "Benjamin!"

"Hey," he said pushing the door open a bit farther. "Do you mind if I come in?"

"Of course not," she laid down her pen and paper. "What are you doing here?"

"I needed to come home," he said walking cautiously into the room toward her.

"Well I am sure your mom missed you."

"That's not my home."

"Benjamin, please don't."

"Danny, you know my home has always been here with you." He was standing in front of her.

She looked up at him, tears forming in her eyes, "Don't. Please."

"I have missed you, even when I didn't know that was what the hole was. I missed you."

"I know why you're home. Everyone does. So please…….."

"I admit it. I fucked up. I always fuck up. But you are always there."

"I can't be. Not after last time. Not anymore."

Benjamin dropped to his knees in front of her and pulled a box from his pocket.

Danny watched him fear in her eyes, "God, no. Please Benjamin, no."

Benjamin reached out and took her hand into his, he looked up into her tear stained eyes, "I love you."

Danny slid down from the bed and knelt in front of him, "No you don't. You…"

"Danny, will you please marry me?"

Tears spilled from her eyes, she shook her head no even as her mouth said, "Yes."

Benjamin opened the box and took the ring out and slid it onto her finger, "It's always been only you. I was just too blind to see that and too stubborn to know that."

Danny looked into his eyes, "And I love you enough to believe that. I have always loved you, sometimes, I loved you too much."

******

The fragile morning light worked its way through the nicotine stained lace curtains of Danny's bedroom. She and Benjamin lay inches apart from one another on the bed. Benjamin woke up and rolled to his side, sitting up he grabbed his cigarettes off the nightstand that was littered with a coked residue enhanced mirror, a razorblade, an over flowing ashtray, an empty bottle of Jack and two shot glasses. He lit up and took a deep draw. He sat the cigarette in the ashtray and rolled back into the bed and wrapped his arms around Danny.

"Morning lovely…….." He interrupted himself as a sense of fear came over him. He rolled her over and saw her blue lips. Panic flooded him. "Danny?" He rubbed at her chest. The panic became a flood of screams, "Danny! God! Oh God! Danny! Help! Someone help! Danny!"

And that is where Nick and Sarah found him. Holding her and screaming. For Benjamin the rest became a nonsensical blur. A blur that whirled and twirled until it found him sitting alone in a chair in the hallway of a hospital. His head was in his hands, the tears, hot as hell, wouldn't stop.

The next thing he knew Gina Marie walked out of a room teary eyed into the hall and hugged Conner who was standing by the door. When did he get here? Was the only thing Benjamin could think as he watched her pull away and whisper something to him. Conner leaned his forehead to hers momentarily. Then slowly, in what Benjamin would later remember the words, 'a synchronicity of love' Gina Marie and Conner pulled apart and looked at Benjamin.

Later on, Benjamin would memorialize those words and that moment. A moment that would be one remembered as a snapshot that burns into a brain, in a song, a song that would be Conner's first number one hit. The song, unlike the lady they would memorialize, would win awards and acclaim.

Slowly the couple walked as one down the hall to him.

When they stood in front of him, he looked up and into Gina Marie's eyes. "I'm sorry Benjamin," is what she said biting back tears.

Benjamin looked at her through tears of his own. His heart was ripping apart. Literally, he could feel physical pain in his chest, he was aware of his heart beating erratically. Slowly he stood.

Gina Marie stepped forward and embraced him, pulling away she uttered, "She was already dead when the paramedics arrived. There was nothing they could do. Nothing anyone could have done."

Benjamin inhaled a deep stale breath of hospital scents. Fresh tears began to roll. Conner stepped forward and embraced him, for a long moment Benjamin held on, then suddenly and without warning Benjamin pulled away. He turned from his friends and walked off down the hall.

******

Death was never something that Benjamin had paid particular attention to. Pets died rather quickly, they were there one day and gone the next, so he had never had one. Never really wanted one. He knew of course, that people died. That's just what they did. Here today, gone home tomorrow. So he had never really allowed himself to feel, to know, or to experience death. Feelings were too risky, too dicey and always ended with him feeling bad or at least be expected to feel bad. So he had made it through his life spreading misery because he refused to allow himself to feel and to acknowledge feelings. A real cold fish he was.

Or so he had thought.

On this morning sometime after Danny had left him, and left him is how he finally convinced himself to look at it, he awoke in a poorly lit trash strewn room with some anonymous female's arm and head across his chest.

He brushed her off with a look of pure disgust and rolled out of bed.

He grabbed a bottle of Jägermeister off the floor and tilted it up sucking the remaining warm liquor out of it. He walked sluggishly out of the bedroom into the trash-filled living room. Tripping several times on his way to the couch, he fell down onto it and righted himself; jerkily he pulled the coffee closer to him. He picked up a razor blade and began scrapping up what was left of last night's high. When he created a bump from the dust he snorted it and then sat there and stared at the razor blade. He looked from it to the veins in one of his arms.

"Oh shit!" He threw the razor blade down and happen to glance at the floor, where sticking out from the mess was a corner of the hot pink CD case. His mind went back to the day he had left it there for Danny. He remembered the sight and the sounds of her then peaceful slumber. Lost in the memory of her he laid back on the couch.

Vaguely he was aware of the sound of running water. The next thing he knew he felt the icy needles of water hitting him. "Fuck!" He screamed.

Slowly he started to fight against the water. Scrambling against the slick tile of the shower. He fell forward out of the shower and onto the bathroom floor. He heard the water shut off, and though afraid to do so, he rolled over and opened his eyes to see Harris sitting on the toilet with a cigarette in his mouth.

"Cold wasn't it?" Were the first words Benjamin was aware of hearing for quite some time.

Like a wounded animal Benjamin curled himself into a fetal position and spat out, "Fuck you!"

Harris calmly stood up and held out his hand to Benjamin who took it and allowed the help to get him off the floor. Standing face to face Benjamin whispers, "What the hell are you doing here?"

"Your entertainment from last night called me when she couldn't wake you up."

Benjamin stared at him coldly, then turned and walked into the living room tripping his way over and through the mess. "How did she know to call you?"

"I did her last week, she knows we're friends." Benjamin just looked at him with a hint of disgust. "Hey, don't be surprised. There are only so many women of our quality level in Nashville. It had to happen sooner or later."

"Yeah. Well, you're free to go whenever." Benjamin slammed himself down into the couch. "Preferably now."

Harris walked over to the litter strewn bar and picked up a container of coffee. "I'm not going anywhere," he said walking over to Benjamin and handing him the coffee.

Benjamin tried to knock the coffee out of Harris' hand, but Harris was faster. "Fucking get out of my house."

Harris grinned and pushed Benjamin backwards as he tried to get up. "You fucking sit down and drink this, or I call in reinforcements."

Benjamin looked at him for a long moment. He reached out and took the coffee, Harris looked around the room and pulled a chair through the mess and sat down in front of him. He looked around the room at the mess, "Nice to see you're still living the dream."

"Oh, please. I have seen your place."

"So, what's with this shit you're pulling?"

"Like you care. You checked out on me a long time ago."

"You can think that if you want to."

"What am I supposed to think? You and Conner walked out on me. Left me stranded."

"Have you not seen one romantic comedy in your life? If you would've followed us and apologized like a man who meant it, things would have been different. A lot different. And I'm sorry for all the shit you dealt with. But it has been no picnic for me and Conner either."

"That's life man, deal with it."

"Are you really going to be an asshole right now, sitting there buck naked and all."

"If it gets you out here, yeah."

"Well asshole away, dude, cause I am not leaving." Benjamin just stared at him. Five minutes passed with Benjamin sipping his coffee and Harris watching. "You know, both of you took using to a whole new level. What happened, well it could have been either of you. And if I hadn't showed up, it would have been both of you."

"Shut up."

"It wasn't your fault man. At least not all of it. She was how much older than you? I mean from the looks of it you're well on your way to joining her. "

"Shut the fuck up."

"You have to ask yourself, is this what she would want for you? I mean, she seemed to work pretty hard to make up better than what I am seeing."

Benjamin stood up, "Fuck you! You didn't even know her! I fucking loved her!" He began to tear up. "I loved her," he managed to croak out before the tears fell like a fresh spring rain.

"I know you did." Harris stood and walked over to put his arms around Benjamin. "And she knows you did too."

Harris stood back, "Okay, Naked Man. Go shower and find something clean to put on we have to get you out of here." Benjamin just looked at him. "Hey, dude you are naked, I am not hugging you again. Now go get dressed."

Benjamin stumbled off toward the bathroom.

EPILOGUE

Pull the Curtain

Benjamin was in the sound booth at The Bomb Shelter, he removed his head phones and smiled out at Gina Marie through the window as he unplugged his guitar. He walked out still smiling. "So was it any good?"

Gina Marie looked at him and smiled, "It was ab fab, sweetie."

"I want to thank you again for the free time."

"It's always here when you need it."

Conner and Harris walked into the studio together as Benjamin was sitting in a chair at the sound board next to Gina Marie.

Harris looked at the two of them, "So Gina, how did it go with that asshole?"

"Just fine."

"Good, cause I have worked with him before and I know he can be difficult."

"Excuse me," Conner said walking past Harris and putting both hands on the arms of Gina Marie's chair he bent down and kissed her. "It's been too long since I've done that."

"It's been six hours at the most."

"And that is entirely too long."

Harris groaned, "Sick. Get a room."

Gina Marie looked up at him, "Excuse me? I own the building."

Harris rolled his eyes, "Whatever."

Gina Marie turned her attention back to Conner, "How was the recording session my lovely?"

"Great. But I missed having you there."

"So how's your album coming?" Benjamin broke in.

"Really good. It is why I came to this city."

Harris patted Conner's back, "our country music star. So you going to tell him or do I?"

"I think I'll let you have the honors sir."

Harris grinned, and looked at Benjamin. "Next Big Nashville wants us, *The Velvet Clutches*."

Benjamin smiles, "They do know that we're not a band anymore, right?"

"We pointed that out. But Harris and I were talking and we thought why not just one more show? I mean, well, in case you don't remember we were one of the first Nashville rock bands to make a half way decent go of it."

"Plus we headlined the first one and you and Conner helped set that one up," added Harris.

Benjamin looked at each of them, "Would you guys really want to do this with me?"

Harris smiled, "It's Exit/In dude. Playing there with my two best friends. Instead of session drumming for some American Idol drama country queen I can't fuck or drink around? Are you really asking me that question?'

Conner looked over at Harris and shook his head, "He and I talked about it and said yes. Now it's up to you."

Benjamin grinned, "Let's do it."

"Cool beans," said Harris.

"I'll call the girl and make it official," said Conner.

THE
FUCKING
END